INVASION!

As Gringo's crew waded ashore and dropped behind what cover they could find, one of the crewmen walked upright toward the limelight, hands high, shouting for mercy. He didn't get much. A fusillade of rifle fire cut him down.

Captain Gringo set up his Maxim, armed it. As others crowded nearby he yelled, "Spread out, use your own guns, damn it! Don't let them nail us all with the same mortar round!"

Turning to the pretty Kanaka island girl at his side he growled, "Atanua, keep your head up and your ass down."

Proudly, the girl said, "Me picked up rifle dropped by dead man. Who you want me to shoot?"

"Cover my right flank and shoot anything trying to come down the beach at us."

Suddenly, a rifle squad charged boldly from that direction. Gringo swung the Maxim's giant muzzle around but held his fire. He waited until they moved within point-blank range. "Now!" he shouted as bullets chewed into the defenders....

Novels by
RAMSAY THORNE

Published by
WARNER BOOKS

Renegade #28

THE SLAVE RAIDERS

Ramsay Thorne

WARNER BOOKS

A Warner Communications Company

The cutting edge of the tropical cloudburst had caught Captain Gringo by surprise on his way back to the hotel that evening. So as it went on raining cats, dogs, and hail outside, the big blond American soldier of fortune was enjoying a sedate soak in a warm tub as his wet duds hung to dry in the next room. Naturally, his shoulder rig was hanging on the knob of the locked bathroom door, since he seldom took either a rubber duck or a double-action .38 in the tub with him. Thus he was chagrined as well as surprised when the door suddenly popped open and a deep she-male voice said, "Oh, *here* you are, Captain Gringo!"

He growled, "And here *you* are, too," as he frowned warily up at his unexpected visitor.

She was a sight to make anyone wary. For while there was no doubt she was all woman and quite attractive; the big broad looming in the doorway had to stand at least six-foot-six. And even though her voluptuous curves filled her white linen blouse and skirts nicely indeed, she had to outweigh him by a good forty pounds!

After that it wasn't so bad. Her ebony hair was piled atop her head Gibson-girl style; so, along with the fashionable outfit suited to tennis or the tropics, she added up to reasonably civilized despite her Apache-brown complexion. Her almond eyes were even friendlier, and her features, while not as out of place in Central America as Captain

1

Gringo's, somehow just missed looking really Latina when one looked twice. She was about twenty-five and quite pretty, but she didn't really work as white, black, or Indian. So what was left? And how the hell had she gotten in through at least two locked doors?

He asked her. She looked down at the knob clutched absentmindedly in one big brown paw and replied, "Oh, was the door locked? I didn't notice. I knocked and knocked. But I guess you didn't hear me because of the hail outside."

He didn't want to argue with anyone that strong, with his gun on the wrong side of those massive hips. So he said, "Well, you're in now. Would you hand me a towel so I can get out?"

She did so, but asked, matter-of-factly, "Why? Are you ashamed of your cock? Not to worry. My royal personage is tapu to commoners."

He laughed as he took the towel, asking, "Don't you mean taboo?" And as he rose from the waves like Venus, wrapping the towel around his naked loins, she wrinkled her nose and answered, "If I'd have *meant* 'taboo' I'd have *said* 'taboo.' I wish you pink people wouldn't insist on explaining our religion to us. Haven't you fucked up your own enough?"

He stepped gingerly out of the tub, noting with some relief that she backed out of the doorway to make room for him instead of swinging at him. As he followed her out into the bedroom of his hotel suite, he nodded thoughtfully and said, "Got it. You're a Sandwich Islander, right?"

She shook her head and said, "Farther south. South of Bora Bora. I just came from my lawyer's. He said that while it's true chattel slavery is illegal in Costa Rica, the local government has no jurisdiction; and my best bet would be to hire my own guns. So here I am."

"You've already said that." He sighed, adding, "Do you always start your stories in the middle, Miss . . . ah?"

"Oh, sorry. I'm Princess Manukai of Konakona. I'm used to being recognized on sight. Back home, people are supposed to get out of my way and pray until I pass."

"I believe they would. How did you make it all the way from the South Pacific without getting as wet as the rest of us common folk, Princess? Are you taboo, I mean tapu to common rain as well?"

She laughed and said, "Silly, I'm staying here at the hotel. I got back from my lawyer and the German consulate before the storm broke. I only learned a few minutes ago the notorious Captain Gringo was a guest here as well."

He rolled the top of the towel so it wouldn't slip when he freed his hands to move over to a sideboard, saying, "I'm having gin and tonic. You?"

She nodded but told him to skip the tonic. So he poured her a straight gin as he mused aloud, "I wish people wouldn't gossip about me in the halls so much, Princess. Just what did they tell you about me that makes me so notorious?"

She sat on the bed, making it sag ominously as she replied demurely, "Just that you're wanted for murder in the States, that you're an ex–U.S. Army officer and ordnance expert who holes up here in Costa Rica between jobs and, oh yes, that your job is killing people for hire, with a machine gun. I can get you a machine gun. I come from a very wealthy family."

He handed her her heroic drink, sat on a nearby bentwood chair with his own less lethal one and said, "Before we go any further with this weird conversation, let's get a few things straight, Princess. Numero uno, I'm a soldier of fortune, not a hired assassin."

"There's a difference? Not to worry. The job I'm

offering is a military invasion. I have about fifty warriors of my own waiting for us aboard my schooner down at Puntarenas. I'm afraid they may be a little unsophisticated for the type of operation I have in mind. So I need officers trained in the art of war as you pink people fight one another. Do you think your little French friend from the Foreign Legion could be persuaded to join us, Captain Gringo?''

He grimaced and said, ''People have been talking a lot to you, I see. Just what did they tell you about old Gaston, Princess?''

She took a healthy belt of gin, as if it were water, and replied, ''Just that his name is Gaston Verrier and that he is a very skilled artillery ace as well as an all-around and deadly soldier of fortune. You two often work as a team, don't you? If you can persuade him to take part in the invasion, I'm sure I can find some field mortars, at least, for him.''

Captain Gringo smiled crookedly and replied, ''You're right. You're rich. And, while we're on the subject, how come you dress like a rich young white chick and speak better English than a lot of them? No offense, Princess, but when you say 'South Sea Islands,' I can't help getting this picture of naked people eating coconuts and one another.''

She sighed and said, ''Oh pooh, you're as bad as the girls I went to school with at Vassar. It's true the *common* people back home are a bit, ah, unspoiled. But honestly, do I look common to you?''

''Not hardly, I heard the queen of the Sandwich Islands has a German band and hot and cold running water in her new palace on Oahu, too. How do you, ah, royals make out so well? Oil wells or something?''

Princess Manukai shook her head and said, ''Konakona ships copra, sugar and, of course, pearl shell, along with some pearls. It's the pearl business that's caused all the trouble. The blackbirders could get all the native help they needed here in Central America if all they were interested in was copra and sugar. Alas, my people are the best pearl divers in the South Pacific, so the blackbirders—"

"Back up!" he cut in, adding: "They taught you English swell at Vassar. But they must have fogotten to tell you it's not a guessing game. Who or what in the hell is a blackbirder?"

She looked blank, then nodded and said, "That's right. You Yankees called them *slavers*. Out our way they're called blackbirders. I don't know why. Our people are neither birds nor black. But the people who grab them are called blackbirders just the same."

He sipped at his own drink with a thoughtful frown as he tried to decide whether she was serious or enjoying an obscure joke at his expense. Then he said, "Come on, Princess, chattel slavery's been outlawed even in Brazil, now. We're almost into the twentieth century. Are you suggesting people are actually being seized as slaves at this late date?"

She said, "Suggesting it, shit, I'm *saying* it! Over a hundred of my people, and others from other islands, are being held as slaves just off the west coast of Central America and, goddamn it, it's got to stop!"

He didn't answer until he'd taken another sip and studied her words some. He knew it was true some local big shots held their peones in little more than simple bondage. He knew primitive Indians were exploited, often at gunpoint; but, hell, there had to be *some* rules.

He said, "Run that bit about the German consulate by me again, Princess. What on earth could young Kaiser Willy have to do with South Sea Island natives being kidnapped to dive for pearl shell off Costa Rica, for God's sake?"

She said, "They deny it at the consulate, too. But the

international company working the pearl beds of the Guardian Bank is still German-owned.''

"Guardian Bank?''

"An archipelago of low coral islands about a hundred miles off the west coast of Costa Rica. The Costa Rican lawyer I spoke to says his government claims no jurisdiction over them.''

"I'm not surprised. This is the first I've heard of them. Are they worth anybody's time and navy, Princess?''

"As islands, no. Most of the Guardian Bank consists of barely submerged reefs, dangerous to and hence avoided by shipping. Only a few of the larger keys remain above water at high tide, and that's not saying much. They're sun-baked, arid sand spits with little vegetation and no fresh water between rains. That's why the people being held there are at the mercy of the pearlers. There's no timber to improvise escape rafts, and no place to hide without food and water. No food and water, in fact, unless one's willing to work from sunrise to sunset for the blackbirders who control all supplies and transportation in or out.''

"How do you know all this, Princess? Have you ever been there?''

"Do I look like a captive vahine? I know the little I do know about conditions there because my people are so brave we even frighten one another at times. One night a Konakona boy who'd taken all he could just started swimming east, hoping to reach the mainland.''

"Jesus, a hundred miles, against the trade winds?''

She shrugged and said, "He'd have never made it, of course. But after he'd swum all night, some decent Costa Rican fishermen spotted him bobbing in the ground swells and brought him ashore. Needless to say, they own a new fishing boat now. The boy spoke no Spanish, of course, but he knew a little English. So the Costa Ricans turned him over to an American missionary in Puntarenas who now runs a bigger mission. The kind mission people put the boy aboard a copra schooner bound for Konakona, and the rest you know. How soon do you intend to put your pants on and help me rescue my people still held captive?''

He grimaced and said, ''I'm not sure we can help you at all, Princess. Gaston and I are *soldiers* of fortune, not buccaneers. Even if we were the navy types I'd say you really need, I'll tell you frankly, we just got paid off for a more sensible-sounding dry-land operation and, well, Costa Rica's one of the few decent countries down here that doesn't have an extradition treaty with either the States or France. I just can't see Gaston and me sticking our necks out that far from shore. Imperial Germany is one country that would *really* like to get its hands on the two of us, and you said yourself the krauts are in control of the Guardian Bank.''

''Don't you want to know what's in it for you if you help me?''

He didn't answer. She put her half-empty glass on the bed table, stood up, and began to unbutton her blouse as she said, ''I can offer you a thousand a week, each, plus a ten-thousand-dollar bonus if we succeed.''

She opened her blouse, exposing a heroic pair of firm brown breasts as she added, ''I can be generous in other ways as well, Captain Gringo.''

He said, ''I'm sure you can. But I thought you just said your royal personage was, ah, tapu?''

She shrugged and began to unfasten her skirts as she said, ''I'm not sure the tapu applies to pink people. Certainly not officers in the Royal Konakona Navy, Captain Gringo.''

''Under the circumstances, call me 'Dick.' I didn't know you had a navy.''

''We didn't, up to now. But if only you'd agree to be

my, ah, admiral, you'd find me as generous, in every way, as your Queen Elizabeth was to her Francis Drake, Dick.''

He laughed and said, "I'm not sure one could call her *my* queen, or that old Bess put out for her royal navy. If she was built at all like you, and did, it's no wonder the Spanish Armada wound up in so much trouble! But hold the thought and don't drop that skirt just yet, Princess. I just said I wasn't sure about signing up with you, remember?''

She let the white linen fall, a long way, to the carpet around her high-button shoes. Then she stepped out of her skirts, wearing nothing but said shoes and thin silk stockings as she asked simply, "Are you still not sure, Dick?''

He was sure he wanted her so bad it hurt, for any man born of mortal woman would have wanted all six-foot-six of anything breathtaking as Princess Manukai of Konakona in the beautiful buff. Despite her size and pneumatic proportions, there wasn't an ounce of flab under all that smooth tawny skin; and the little V between her hula hips would have looked yummy indeed had she been less than perfection elsewhere. But Captain Gringo was alive that evening because, in the past, he'd learned the hard way to think with his head instead of his glands. So he silently warned his sudden erection to behave itself as he told the princess, aloud, "I said to hold the thought.''

"Don't you . . . want me, Dick?''

"Do I look sick or celibate, Honey? What I want or don't want is not the point. The point is, I can't commit myself to anything until I've talked it over with my sidekick and, frankly, checked you out.''

"Why don't you start with a physical examination, then? That's not a gun you're pointing at me from under that towel is it?''

He laughed and said, "You know damned well what it is, and we both know what you're trying to pull off here, aside from my poor teased pecker. You know damned well I'd promise you the moon, once we got to know each other even better. But it's not my style to break my word or to get my fool self killed trying to keep it. So . . . look, you said you're staying in this hotel, right?''

"Room two-oh-seven." She sighed, bending over, way over, to pull her skirts back up as she observed, "They *told* me you were a man of iron, damn it. How soon may I expect to hear from you, one way or the other?''

He said, "As soon as I make up my mind, of course," as he wistfully watched her put her clothes back on.

When she had, she said, "Don't take too long. You're not the only soldier of fortune in these parts, you know."

He nodded and said, "Forgive me for not rising," as she moved to let herself out, observing with a becoming blush, "I see you already have."

They both laughed like mean little kids. And then she was gone but hardly forgotten. He got up to lock the hall door after her. He couldn't. Like the bathroom door, it was ruined forever. He jiggled the broken knob, sighed, and said, "It figures," as he tried to decide what on earth he'd tell the hotel handyman when he asked to have both doors fixed. He wondered what good it would do to fix either. Obviously, Princess Manukai was too strong to be kept out by mere hotel locks. But so far, thank God, she seemed to be a *friendly* native. He wondered what she acted like when she got pissed off at someone. He didn't think he wanted to find out.

Gaston didn't want to find out either. When the dapper little Frenchman returned to the hotel, sensibly, after the storm let up as suddenly as it had begun, Captain Gringo naturally filled him in on the strange princess and her strange offer, leaving out the dirty parts near the end. Just as naturally, the American member of the team had put his own clothes back on by then. So Gaston's first suggestion was, "Eh bien, let us make the tracks. Royal personages who twist off doorknobs with their bare hands make me très nervous, and I know another posada here in San Jose where not even our mothers could find us, hein?"

Captain Gringo stared soberly without answering as he digested Gaston's words of wisdom. Gaston was over twenty years older than Captain Gringo and, as he never tired of explaining, had gotten to *be* that old in a danger- ous game because he'd learned in his youth not to needlessly buck the odds. Gaston must have taken his younger comrade's silence as disagreement, since he insisted, "Merde alors, it is too big a species of boo, Dick! The young woman may or may not have money, a schooner, even a modest handful of her own très savage warriors to, how you say, back her play? But I *do* know the Guardian Bank. I was almost stranded there once, and once was more than enough! Should anything go wrong, and I see nothing *right* about her simple plan, we would wind up most stuck, a hundred miles out to sea, on a très unfriendly shore indeed! Aside from mysterious German slavers infesting the barren little bits of rock, the Guardian Bank can kill you with no help from anyone! There is no food, no water, and because of the treacherous reefs around the few islets, no hope of a passing vessel putting in to rescue one's adorable ass! The whole thing sounds like a disaster waiting for fools to walk into it and—Why the bemused smile, my old and rare? Was she really that good-looking?"

Captain Gringo sighed and said, "Nobody's that good- looking. When you make sense, you make sense. I'll tell her the deal's off."

Gaston asked, "Why? Do you really wish to witness a

six-foot-six temper tantrum, Dick? Let her figure it out for herself once we are no longer on the premises, hein? There are plenty of other places for us to stay here in San Jose, and she was right about there being plenty of other soldiers of fortune in town as well. At the price she's offering, she'll have no trouble recruiting some maniacs and—''

''That's one of the things that's making me feel shitty,'' Captain Gringo cut in, going on to explain; ''The poor kid's already been all over town talking to lawyers and, Jesus, even the German consul. She found me in the first place by asking around town for some handy guys at gunplay. So by now, unless they don't have a friend at all in this neck of the woods, that German-run pearling syndicate has to know just what her plans are!''

Gaston nodded and said, ''But of course. That is one of the main reasons I regard her scheme as too dangerous. The princess, and anyone she hires to invade whatever species of islet her people are being held on, has no idea what may be waiting for them there. The so-called blackbirders could be on any of a dozen keys with any sort of defensive setup, and worse yet, they already know she's coming, avec what! She has not the chance of the snowball in hell, Dick!''

Captain Gringo nodded grimly and said, ''I just said you were right. I just wish I knew some way to make *her* see it. She seems like a good kid, in a sort of weird way. But every time I try to tell her the idea doesn't sound so hot, she just starts to take her clothes off.''

Gaston brightened and said, ''Oh? You left the good parts out, I see! Is that why you hesitate to escape with me, my horny child? Having enjoyed the gigantic favors of the maiden in distress, you feel some très grotesque obligation to die for her?''

''Don't talk like an asshole, you asshole. I turned *that* proposition down too, and it wasn't easy. It's just that . . . Aw shit, let's get out of here before I have to face her again. It's just a no-win situation no matter what I tell her.''

"Eh bien, let us be on our cowardly way then. This posada I mentioned earlier, I neglected to say, comes with hot and cold running women even if the plumbing leaves something to be desired. The best cure I can think of for a six-foot-six vahine would be a Spanish redhead in the neighborhood of five-foot-two with eyes of blue, non?''

Captain Gringo laughed, agreed, and since they'd checked in with no luggage in the first place, they went down the back stairs to check out the least complicated way. They'd paid for their rooms in advance, been overcharged, so who cared about the busted doors, right?

That would have been the end of it. Princess Manukai might or might not have found someone else, and either succeeded or failed on her own. But since the night was still young—for a Latin American night—and on sober reflection Gaston couldn't swear for certain about there being all that many dames at the other posada across town, the two soldiers of fortune stopped at the main plaza near the cathedral to drink some cerveza and reconsider their options.

The early unexpected rain naturally had put a damper on the sunset paseo. So, as naturally, once things had dried out before midnight, the plaza was once more filled with strolling players of opposing sexes looking for sex, although nobody was about to admit it.

The way the Latin American paseo was supposed to work was that the girls circled the plaza one way and the boys circled it the other, so everyone got to pass everyone of the other gender over and over as one and all pretended they weren't interested. Older and wiser hands like Captain Gringo and Gaston had learned it made as much sense conquest-wise, and even more, exercise-wise, to just stay put at a sidewalk cantina table under a hanging lantern and let the passing muchachas see for themselves how pretty you were and, more important, that you had drinking money and weren't desperate. El Paseo was always run lady's choice. A guy who smiled at a woman first was considered an uncouth sex maniac and, worse yet, a country boy or a married john without time to spend on a real romance.

If a muchacha was looking to get picked up, and there'd be little point in all that walking if she weren't, she'd let you know, the fifth or sixth time your eyes met in passing, that she was aware of your existence. If she didn't fancy you, she wouldn't notice you on the last night of her life. But, on the other hand, since she'd never noticed you in the first place, she'd never actually *snub* you. So there was a lot to be said for El Paseo, in contrast with the crueler way the game was played up north.

Back in the States, a Victorian Maiden Fair expected the poor slob to approach her; and so a lot of awkward, homely guys left every dance feeling even more awkward and ugly while a lot of she-male wallflowers got to go home feeling like losers as well. At El Paseo even the Hunchback of Notre Dame, male or female, was left with their dignity, at least, intact. One could always assume the "stroller" one admired was simply too shy to make eye contact; and so, while just as many ugly boys and girls struck out, they never felt humiliated.

Neither Captain Gringo nor Gaston struck out too often. The big blond American was attractive at a glance to most women. Gaston, though older, smaller, and grayer, could be considered nice-looking on second glance; and all clean-looking foreigners intrigued the older and more adventurous women of any nationality. So the two of them were just sitting there, idly watching the proceedings, when a couple of burly blancos in linen suits that could have used some laundry soap sat down at their tin table with them, uninvited.

This alone was a serious insult in Hispanic circles. But since neither they nor the two soldiers of fortune seemed to be Hispanic, Captain Gringo just smiled thinly and asked them what they wanted.

The bigger of the pair, who also could have used a shave, said flatly, "We want you guys to butt out, see?"

Captain Gringo just stared coldly at them. Gaston said, "You must have us confused with someone else, mon ami. We just got here. We have yet to be smiled at by even one of the passing throng. So if you wish to be inside the track with any particular species of femme in the vicinity, just point her, or them, out and . . ."

"That's not what I'm talking about and you know it, Frog Face," cut in the bully with a knowing sneer.

His pal nodded and said, "Yeah, who're you trying to shit? Do we look stupid or sumpin'?"

Gaston smiled fondly and said, "You would know better than I how stupid you look, since it is your face, not mine, you see in the mirror on the rare occasions you may choose to shave, hein?"

Captain Gringo said, "Cut the comedy, Gaston. You guys may as well cut it too. Is there any point to all this bullshit, or are you two just looking for a fight?"

"Whaddaya, some kind of tough guy, Walker?"

"If you know my name, you know better than to start up with me like a pair of peon punks baiting a tourist. You both look like Yanks. So let's all talk plain English. What do you want, if it's not our boots?"

The smaller of the two, which wasn't saying tiny, nudged his even burlier companion and growled, "Jeez, don't he talk brave, Spike?" And Spike growled back, "Yeah, they tol' us he was brave. They tol' us to watch out for the shiv the little frog carries sneaky under the back of his shirt collar, too.''

Captain Gringo turned to Gaston to say in a conversational tone, ''I'll take the big one, okay?''

Gaston shrugged and said, ''Spoilsport. My little sister could kick the merde out of either, in her ballet slippers. But go ahead and amuse yourself with M'seau Spike if you wish. I'll just watch. The other one is all mouth.''

Captain Gringo took off his wide-brimmed Panama and placed it on the table. But before he could rise, the one called Spike said, ''Hey, wait, don't you want to hear the message we brung you?''

''You brought us a message? I thought you just enjoyed living dangerously, Spike?''

''Jeez, ain't you got no sense of humor? The guys that sent us tol' us to tell you to stay the hell away from that big Hawaiian dame, see?''

''I'm beginning to. Who sent you, Spike?''

The professional tough grinned knowingly and replied, ''Wouldn't you like to find out?''

''I sure would, Spike. So now you're going to tell me, aren't you?''

Spike shook his head and said, ''Naw, they tol' us not to, uh, go inta details. They tol' us to just tell you to stay away from the dame and out of the game if you know what's good for you.''

As they both rose, the smaller one said, ''You know what's good for you, don't you, Walker?''

Captain Gringo glanced at Gaston and raised an eyebrow. The Frenchman nodded and said, ''Oui, let's get it out of them.'' So Captain Gringo put his hat back on, both soldiers of fortune rose, and the two tough-looking thugs started running as if their lives depended on it.

It did. None of the Costa Ricans all around saw fit to interfere as, for some strange blanco reason, two gringo lunatics seemed to be chasing two other gringo lunatics down one side of the plaza. Spike and his pal knew their way around San Jose, too. So, long before they got near the police post down at the southwest corner, they cut into a westbound alley to really start picking them up and laying them down as Spike panted, "Jeez, Pud, did you have to dare them like that? We was only paid to lay the word on 'em, you asshole!"

Pud panted back, "Keep running, dammit! Walker's *gaining* on us!"

Actually, Captain Gringo wasn't running as fast as he could as he paced the frightened toughs the length of the block-long alley. For guys who talked so rugged, it was obvious neither was in real shape. So he chased them just hard enough to keep them looking back as, meanwhile, Gaston did some more serious running via another route and, just as Spike and Pud thought they'd made the end of the alley and were wondering where to run next, Gaston made their minds up for them by materializing in *front* of them to shout, "Boo!"

That naturally froze them, as planned. So as Gaston gaily kicked Spike in the balls and then kicked him in the face when he doubled over, Captain Gringo pounced on Pud like a cat, picked him up by the scruff of the neck and the seat of the pants, and tried to see if Pud's head were harder than the stucco-covered bricks of the nearest wall.

It wasn't. Captain Gringo dropped the limp, unconscious Pud at his feet, stepped over him, and said, "Gaston, don't kick old Spike any more. He's going to tell us a story, ain't that right, Spike?"

Spike just lay on his side, groaning as he clutched his groin with both hands. So Captain Gringo kicked him in the ribs. Gaston muttered, "That is not fair, Dick. You had your own dolly to play with. Must you take mine as well?"

Captain Gringo said, "I think I broke my dolly. This one can still talk, if it knows what's good for it. Do you know what's good for you, Dolly?"

Spike moaned, "Jeez! Don't kick me no more! Jus' gimme a sec to get my fuckin' breath back, okay?"

Captain Gringo kicked him in the shins this time and said, "You can breathe all you want after you tell us who sent you. *Talk*, you shit-heel!"

"Hey, what can I tell you? It was just a guy, a knockaround guy we met in a cantina near the depot earlier tonight. He tol' us your names and tol' us what to tell you. He might have warned us you was so tough, the motherfucker!"

Captain Gringo kicked him again and growled, "Flattery will get you nowhere, you lying bastard. If you're knockaround guys from San Jose, you already heard about Gaston and me. You want to try again, or do you think the girls would admire you more with your face kicked in?"

"Okay! Okay! We heard your reps around town, but nobody tol' us how short-tempered you guys was, for Chrissake! We was just supposed to warn you away from that hula-hula dancer. Nobody said nothing about starting up with you and getting ourselves half-killed!"

"I'm waiting to hear the name of the guy who sent you, Spike."

"What can I tell you? He was just a guy-type guy, and—Don't kick me again, damn it! He never laid his name on us. He just laid twenty bucks each on us and tol' us to make sure you got his message loud and clear!"

"We got his message. I'm still waiting to hear more about *him*, Spike."

Before Spike could answer, Gaston hissed, "Regard!" and pushed Captain Gringo to one side as, drawing his own .38, he put a bullet in Pud as the dazed but armed and dangerous thug rose to his feet and, naturally, went right back down again.

As Pud's own revolver clattered to the cobbles, Captain Gringo said, "Thanks," drew his own revolver, and said, "That shot's sure to draw the law, so we haven't time for more games, Spike. The name—now. I won't ask again!"

Spike pleaded, "Don't! I swear I don't know the guy's name. He was just a . . . Wait, he had an accent, like he was a Swede or maybe a Dutchman, and—"

In the distance, a police whistle was blowing. So Captain Gringo nodded and said, "Let's get out of here, Gaston."

Gaston said, "Oui, lead on, MacDuff," as he aimed the .38 in his hand and cold-bloodedly blew off the side of Spike's head.

As the two of them ran out of the alley, slowed down near the corner, and strolled around it together innocently, Captain Gringo asked, "Why did you have to do that? I think the poor slob was telling the truth."

Gaston nodded and said, "So do I. But I remember my dear old Aunt Mimi telling me one time, as she was going sixty-nine with me, never to leave a witness to a killing behind."

Captain Gringo sighed and said, "She had a point. Sorry. Wasn't thinking. We'd better get off the street poco tiempo. Spike wasn't the only witness who can place us near the *first* slob you had to shoot. A whole plaza full of people saw us chase them down that alley!"

"True, but what can they say, save that two men dressed less like natives were chasing two others? Fortunately, all four of us left the paseo before anyone who knows us well here in San Jose stopped to have a drink with us. So who can connect us with two tramps we never met before, hein?"

"The guy who sicced them onto us, for one. We still don't know who he might have been, and he knew who we were and where to *find* us, before we even *got* there!"

"Merde alors, do you have to be so cheerful as midnight approaches, Dick? We'd better swing right at the next corner if we intend to make that posada I told you about before the usual tedious police dragnet begins.''

Captain Gringo shook his head and said, ''No. We're going back to the hotel. It's closer, we never checked out in the first place, officially, and the cops never bother people in the classier parts of town.''

''True, my bright pupil on the run. But have you considered that the species of insect that wishes us to stay away from Princess Manukai knows we've been staying at that hotel?''

''I have. By morning he'll have gotten the message we left for him in that alley back there, too. So we'd better cut out early for Puntarenas with old Manukai.''

''Merde alors! You intend to help her after all? I thought we agreed her scheme was sheer lunacy, Dick!''

''It probably is. On the other hand, some prick I don't even know just told me to butt out, and I've always hated to take orders.''

Gaston nodded soberly and said, ''Eh bien, count me in too.''

Since they hadn't checked out, they didn't have to check back in. But since the hall door of Captain Gringo's suite had naturally not been repaired, they slipped into Gaston's digs next door to fort up for the moment as they considered their options.

The second floor of the first-class hotel was laid out in a big H. So there was no way to cover the stairwell and all the corridor ends from Gaston's doorway. Captain Gringo was trying to, holding the door ajar as Gaston started to ''unpack'' by emptying the bulging pockets of his linen jacket atop the bed table. Captain Gringo said, "Hold it. We may have to leave again in a hurry. I'd better run a quick patrol of all the broom closets and, once it looks safe, have a word with the princess."

Gaston took out his pocketknife as he said, "Eh bien, kiss her once for me. Meanwhile, I'll see if I can fix the locks she broke with her très dainty bare hands. I still don't see how she could have done it."

Captain Gringo said, "You still haven't *seen* the dame." But Gaston insisted, "I still don't believe any human being could be that strong. Most hotel locks are cheap, as any good jewel thief can tell you. Mais the cheapest lock is still made of metal and, eh bien, I'll have a look at your abused hotel hardware with my sweet little screwdriver blade. She probably just took advantage of a loose screw, hein?"

Captain Gringo drew his .38 from its shoulder rig, held it in the right side pocket of his jacket, and tossed his hat on Gaston's bed before stepping innocently out into the hall.

He moved to the stairwell and went up to the top. The hotel was four stories tall. A chump might have started his sweep with the fourth floor. But Captain Gringo had hidden out on rooftops himself in the past. So he unscrewed the Edison bulb near the roof exit, popped open the sheet-metal door, and crabbed quickly to one side in case anyone was covering the far side.

Nobody was. The flat roofing all around was dimly illuminated by the sky glow of San Jose. He only had to circle the stairwell shed and water tower once to make sure there were no Apache encampments to worry about up there.

He moved back down the stairs faster than he'd come up them. A house-to-house fighting trick they'd never taught him at West Point regarding stairs was "Up slow, down fast!'' Like a lot of military skills, it made little sense until one thought about it. Then one wondered why one had never thought of that before. A guy moving *up* popped his eyes over an edge while the rest of him was still covered and so might manage to catch someone on a floor above by surprise. But a guy sneaking *down* had his entire body in full view before his eyes could see what the hell he was sneaking down at. Ergo, his chances were better, lousy as they still were, if he simply popped into view all at once.

Nobody was waiting in ambush for him on the fourth-floor landing or around any corners. It occurred to him as he was checking out the third floor that he was probably wasting his time. But he had plenty of time, and while there was no way to make sure some sneak hadn't simply checked into one of the other rooms of the big hotel, at least he made sure nobody was forted up in a broom closet or the bathrooms shared by the guests in the cheaper rooms.

There were no guest facilities below the second floor. The main floor below was taken up by the lobby, bar, dining room, kitchen, stable, storage, quarters for the hotel help, etc. There was no way to check down there without answering a lot of questions he didn't want anyone even asking. There was no way to check the hotel register. Even if he got the room clerk to show him the book, the names on it would mean nothing to him, while at the same time, his curiosity could alert a sneak checked in as ''John Smith'' to the fact that someone was curious about his signature. A night clerk who'd talk to one guest for a modest bribe would talk to any other for the same. He might even *volunteer* the information, in hopes of a tip.

There was nobody even taking a crap in the coed john on the second floor. As he crossed the north-south corridor, he saw Gaston down at the far end kneeling in the doorway of his own room, futzing with the busted lock. He silently

signaled his intent to move on around the corner to the big
dame's suite and did so. The door marked "207" covered
this wing's corridor nicely, he noticed. Anyone meaning to
rush it would have to just rush it head on. He was out to
comfort, not assassinate, the princess, so he simply knocked.

She must have thought he was Room Service, because
she called out "Entrada" from the other side as he heard
her bedsprings add that she was rising to the occasion. He
took the knob in his free hand and twisted. The knob
turned swell. It didn't seem to be connected to anything.
He grinned as the door opened almost by itself. Doors did
that when they had their latches broken off inside.

It was dark in Princess Manukai's suite. It was just as
well. The huge girl was stark-naked, and it wasn't *that*
dark. She said, "Oh, it's you."

He asked, "Who were you expecting?" and she said,
"Nobody. I thought maybe you were one of the hotel help.
Come on in."

He ducked inside and closed the door after him. There
was still enough light to make out her darker nipples and
fetching V of pubic hair as he asked conversationally, "Do
you always greet Room Service in the buff, Doll?"

She sighed and said, "I wasn't thinking. I'm too upset;
and back home, of course, we royal personages don't have
to worry about such things. Our servants know better than
to look at our tapu parts. I'd offer you a drink if I hadn't
finished the bottle. I've been trying to get drunk. It isn't
easy when one has a lot on her mind."

He was too polite to observe that his own considerable
body mass gave him a pretty good capacity for booze,
since she was even bigger, albeit built sissier. He said,
"You can stop worrying, a little at least. We talked it over
and we're in. We're probably nuts, too. But we can worry
about that part later."

The princess gasped with delight, grabbed him in a big,

brown bear hug, and kissed him passionately—almost too passionately. He wasn't used to dames with such big tongues, and even if he had been, who really wanted his tonsils licked? He felt even sillier when the big dame scooped him up in her strong arms and proceeded to carry him over to the bed. He gasped, "Hey, take it easy! Let me get used to this idea before . . ." And then he laughed like hell as he realized what he was saying and who usually said it to *him*! He laughed even harder when the princess lowered him gently to the mattress and said soothingly, "Just relax, Darling. I won't hurt you."

She didn't. But he still felt oddly nervous, excited, and silly as she proceeded to undress him while feeling him up. He was gaining interesting insights that would doubtless come in handy the next time he was in the usual dominant position with somebody smaller than him. But he still didn't feel really she-male, so he started feeling her up as well.

There certainly was an awful lot to feel, and he still felt like he was in more trouble than he might have planned that evening. But there was no doubt she was all dame. So once she had his clothes off, he attempted to reclaim his masculinity by rolling her on her broad brown back. She let him. She probably wanted to feel female. Obviously he'd have never in this world been able to *force* the giant princess into any position she wasn't interested in being in!

But once he was above her in the dim light, with her huge tawny thighs open in welcome, the situation seemed more normal. She even sighed like a shy young thing as he entered her. Captain Gringo had been told by more than one woman he was hung like a horse. He felt like a dirty schoolboy of, say, twelve trying to screw Teacher after school, until the big broad's gaping love maw, proportioned to the rest of her, clamped down politely—almost too tightly for comfort—and all hell broke loose.

It wasn't clear, as she lapsed into crooning Kanaka, whether they were committing "Nukinuki!" or "Poipoi!" or just trying to wreck the joint while Captain Gringo held on for dear life. Princess Manukai, in turn, held on to his erection with her astounding vaginal muscles as in every other way she tried to throw him at the ceiling with fantastic gyrations of her huge, excited pelvis.

She moaned, "Oh, you're so big, the way I like my men!" as she bounced him atop her like a confused rag doll. It helped when she hugged him, topside, against her big brown breasts, either one of which would have been enough for Miss Lillian Russell, according to the *Police Gazette*. He came in her almost at once, or at any rate as soon as he got over his first fright. She seemed not to notice as she went on bumping and grinding or maybe doing the hula-hula on her back. But she must have noticed she was doing all the work now. So she rolled him over on his own back, without a word of warning; and the next thing Captain Gringo knew, he was being treated as a mere sex object. He wasn't sure if he liked it. But there wasn't much he could *do* about it as the big brute vented her lust atop him. At least it didn't hurt, and, yeah, some of the things dames had said to him made more sense to him now.

Like most men, particularly men raised in the Victorian tradition, Captain Gringo had been led to feel that a lot of male-female notions were simply the nature of the critters. So like most men, he tended to be confused as well as annoyed by the sudden mood changes of the sex he now realized literally *was* the weaker sex, most of the time.

Since men were expected to make the first pass and take the lead from that point forward, the male lover had, from first eye contact, an unconscious sense of control and actual physical *safety*. Without thinking, let alone worrying about it, a man at all interested in any woman—any woman smaller than Princess Manukai at any rate—was always in the position to call the whole thing *off* if the party started to get too rich for his blood.

But as he now observed philosophically, from his new perspective, the boldest sex-crazed female had a lot to worry about from the moment she first fluttered her fan. For once the ball was in the air, she was up against someone bigger and stronger who might not know *how* to tickle her fancy but was going to tickle it anyway if she didn't watch her step. So even when a lady wanted to get laid, as he'd wanted to when he knocked demurely on this one's door, the loss of *control* involved was a little scary no matter how good it felt.

But he was starting to relax and feel good indeed as Princess Manukai kept screwing hell out of him. Her legs were so long she had one knee folded down over either side of the mattress, big bare feet on the floor, as she moved her wide-open crotch skillfully up and down the full length of his turgid shaft. Her upper body was braced on her elbows to politely keep most of her weight off his chest, save for her delightfully dangling nipples. This time, when he ejaculated up into her, she felt it and sighed, "Oh, thank you. I'm so glad you're not a single-shot sissy, Dick. Most of you pink people seem to be, for some reason."

He moved his still semi-inspired love machinery inside her teasingly as he asked, in the same conversational tone, "Have you done this with lots of white guys, Doll Box?"

She said, "Not really. I had a missionary back on the island when I was fourteen. He drowned himself later, for some reason. But I hardly got to screw *anyone* until my father sent me to the States for my education. Our commoners get to screw all the time, but we royal personages just have so many tapu restrictions on who we can even *eat* with that it's just not fair!"

"You mean you don't get in on all those native greetings when the fleet's in?"

"Tangaroa, no! We're not supposed to let the commoners even watch us fuck each *other*! The first thing I intend to do, once I'm queen, will be to change some of our sillier customs. Your missionaries are awfully silly. But Tapu can be carried too far, too. I'm not even sure what the kahunas will say when I tell them I've been fucking you pink boys on the mainland. There are so many rules, one just can't keep track."

"Jesus, you're asking me to join a Polynesian navy, and you say I might have just screwed out of bounds, Princess?"

She started screwing him indeed, breathing a little faster, as she replied calmly enough, considering, "Don't call us Polynesians. We're Kanakas. And I just said I don't know if this nice little cock of yours is tapu or not. The kahunas, or high priests, say it's death for a commoner to even *touch* a member of the royal clan. But they never told me, when my father sent me to Vassar, it was tapu to fuck anyone who wasn't a common *Kanaka*, see?"

He chuckled fondly up at her and said, "I sure do. It would have been dumb of you to ask your religious leaders before you got off that frustrating island of yours, wouldn't it?"

She didn't answer. She was resting her big breasts harder against his chest and panting with renewed passion as she moved her big brown derriere faster. It felt good to him, too. But, Jesus, wasn't the brute ever going to stop and let a girl get her breath back, for Pete's sake?

He didn't get to find out. They both heard Gaston's knock on the unlocked and indeed unlockable door. Captain Gringo told her, "Hold it. That's Gaston, and he wouldn't be bothering us just for the hell of it."

If she heard him, she didn't care. She was moaning in protracted orgasm as she tried to drive his ass through the bedsprings with her powerful pubic thrusts. Out in the hall, Gaston had heard enough to take it as his entrance cue. So he came on in to stand there with a doorknob in one hand, bemused, while the couple on the bed went on making love. Or at least as Princess Manukai kept pounding, hard. Captain Gringo looked up at Gaston, red-faced, and said, "Goddamn it, Gaston . . ."

The little Frenchman drew up a hotel chair and sat down calmly, saying, "This is important. You children go ahead and finish coming. I'll find a book to read or something, hein?"

Captain Gringo laughed despite himself and told the princess, "No shit, Doll. Can't we stop a minute?"

Apparently they couldn't. Captain Gringo sighed and said to Gaston, "Forgive me for not rising. May I present Her Highness, Princess Manukai of Konakona?"

Gaston said, "Enchanté, M'selle. Dick, have a look at the disgusting bowels of your door lock."

"*How*, for God's sake? Jesus, Manukai, haven't you had enough for now?"

Gaston chuckled and said, "Obviously she has not, you fortunate devil. Perhaps I can simply explain the matter to you. One hopes he has your attention in part, at least, since time may be of the essence. I see, now, why you said our adorable princess here looked strong enough to you to account for the mangling of steel with her dainty bare hands. But I was right. Some species of sneak had replaced vital parts with *wood*. Packing-case white pine, I would judge from the look of it. Naturally, painted gray and rubbed down with graphite to look like the original metal. My own sweet door was fixed the same way. Since I only have human strength, I would not have noticed had not I really put my back into twisting the knob just now."

Captain Gringo frowned and said, "Jesus, you mean . . . Cut it out, Manukai!"

Gaston nodded soberly and replied, "I mean the doors to all *three* of our suites had been doctored to work normally under normal pressures, to give us all a false sense of security as we locked ourselves in for the night. They probably mean to hit around four A.M. That is the usual time for such events, non?"

This time neither the princess nor Captain Gringo answered. For in her climactic pounding, Manukai had managed to snap something vital holding the bedsprings together and, still coming, crash the whole works to the floor with a thud that shook the whole room!

Gaston laughed—rather rudely, Captain Gringo thought. Then he laughed too as the big brown naked Kanaka girl sat up like a baby in its playpen, still on him, to look around sort of bewildered and ask, "Oh dear, what happened?"

Captain Gringo said, "I wish you'd either slide off my dong or move some more, Honey. Forget what I just said. We may have to make some other good moves right now. Did you hear anything Gaston was just saying?"

She answered, "Who's Gaston?" And then, spotting the sardonic little Frenchman seated by the ruined bedstead regarding them both in a fatherly way, she fluttered her lashes coyly and said, "Oh, I'm so embarrassed. I fear I was overcome with passion just now."

So Captain Gringo reintroduced her to Gaston as she rose in naked majesty to offer Gaston her hand as she stepped grandly over the bed rail. The Frenchman rose to take her hand and kiss it as Captain Gringo sat up, decided nothing was broken but the bed, and muttered, "I wish I could wake up. This dream is getting really silly. What if the hotel just uses unusually cheap locks, even for Bananaland, Gaston?"

As the princess moved demurely into her own bathroom, Gaston shook his head and said, "Two reasons, Dick. In the first place, it would not be cheaper, it would simply be stupider to have some local craftsman make a Chinese copy of an already cheap Connecticut lock in softwood. In the second place, I took the liberty of twisting some other knobs as I made my weary way along the corridor. We three, and we three alone, have been honored with door locks even a child, or at least a Polynesian princess, could open with a single snap!''

Captain Gringo climbed out of the wreckage to fish a claro from his shirt on the floor as he said, ''They prefer to be called Kanakas. Everything else you said makes sense. Up to a point, anyway. To switch locks on us, they'd have to be working with the hotel help, right?''

Gaston shook his head again and said, ''I already thought of the passkey they'd find simpler if it was an inside job. It only took me a few minutes to unscrew the bolt plate and fish out the ruined innards of the adorable devices. Then I had to figure out what all that merde inside *was*! A professional sneak, with a lookout positioned on the stairs, would only need a few seconds to change the locks with ones he'd prepared in advance, hein?''

''What about our keys fitting the original locks? Never mind. Stupid question.''

Gaston answered it anyway, saying, ''Eh bien, *any* key fitted to the same brand of lock will open any lock of species once a small, unimportant plate is removed. As to obtaining the same brand in advance—''

''I just said it was a dumb question,'' Captain Gringo cut in, lighting his claro before he added, ''The only question now is our next move.''

Before Gaston could reply, the princess came out of her bath wearing a kimono and looking contented as only a freshly milked cow or a woman who's just come more than once ever looks. Captain Gringo told Gaston to hold the thought as he scooped up his clothes and ducked into

the john a moment to wash off and dress. It only took a
few minutes, so he was surprised as hell to come out and
find Manukai seated, kimono open, with her long brown
legs hooked over the arms of the chair as Gaston knelt
before her, stripping off his own duds as he ate her pussy.

Captain Gringo muttered, "Oh, for God's sake," as the
big and most obviously uninhibited princess smiled up at
him to say, "I just asked him if it was true what they said
about Frenchman, Dick. I didn't expect him to give me a
practical demonstration so suddenly!"

Captain Gringo grimaced and said, "I can see he
overpowered you. Okay, Kiddies, try not to bust any more
furniture while I see about getting us all to Puntarenas
aboard the last night train. We sure as hell don't want to be
here around four A.M."

They didn't answer. Gaston couldn't talk with his mouth
full, and the princess was starting to breathe funny as she
lay back in the chair to enjoy what might or might not be a
new sensation for a Kanàka world-traveler.

As he left the hotel via the back entrance again, Captain
Gringo began to feel more coolheaded. It wasn't simply
because the night air was cooler after midnight. He'd
started to think cooler about the warm nature of the big
South Sea Island gal. There was no sense getting steamed
about old Gaston going down for sloppy seconds. At least
it hadn't been the other way around; and he'd been a little
worried about anyone that big taking a possessive shine to
him.

At least he shouldn't have to worry now about her
beating him for looking at another woman. She was as bad
as, hell, a *man* about sex. So, yeah, maybe they'd be able
to treat her as one of the boys. She sure was *tougher* than
most of them.

The hotel, catering mostly to out-of-towners, was only a
short walk from the San Jose railroad depot and yards. He

didn't approach the depot via the front entrance. A knockaround guy could get killed doing dumb things like that, even when he didn't know for sure someone was gunning for him for some reason.

He mulled over possible motives as he moved down a side street, found the gap in the fencing he remembered—between two pepper trees nowhere near a street lamp—and eased himself into the dark and, he hoped, deserted rail yards. No yard bulls should be patrolling this close to the depot where no tempting freight cars were standing. He clung to a long black shaft of shadow running in line with the tracks leading to the passenger loading platform ahead, walking slowly to keep from crunching railroad ballast under his mosquito boots as he pondered all the mysterious events of the past few hours.

They refused to make much sense. The princess hadn't even approached him until the sun had sunk mighty low for planning sneaky in advance, so... Wait, she'd said she'd been asking around town all *day*, maybe longer; so, yeah, someone might have guessed she'd meet up with him and Gaston sooner or later at her own hotel and that sooner or later she'd recruit two known soldiers of fortune for her wild rescue scheme.

Okay, the two thugs he and Gaston had taken out *after* the locks must have been doctored had *said* someone didn't want her enslaved subjects rescued, so... That didn't work.

Why would anyone with a lick of sense want to alert a couple of known professional fighting men they might be in trouble if the *real* intent was to hit them harder, later?

Nobody around here figured to explain the riddle to him. So he moved on. He eased up the steps to the platform. If nobody spooky-looking was in the waiting room to cover the front entrance, he'd simply have to step in through the platform entrance and pick up three train rides at the all-night ticket window inside.

He didn't. As he made sure his own face was shadowed and peeked through the grimy glass of a platform window, he saw four guys in the waiting room—waiting for something serious, judging from the way their jackets bulged under the left armpits. All four were dressed blanco. It was too murky inside to make out for sure what probable nationality went with the North American or European duds they wore. Two were seated on opposing benches, covering the front entrance from a cross-fire position. Another sat with his back to Captain Gringo, in position to blast anyone coming in the other way, head on. The fourth, who was either in command or just nervous, was pacing back and forth inside. When he moved over to peek at the deserted street out front, Captain Gringo took off before he could consider the back platform windows.

Captain Gringo slipped out of the rail yards even more confused than he'd slipped in. Scouting the depot had just been the normal precaution that a guy living on the run had to take. He hadn't really expected to *find* such an obvious ambush set up there.

"Maybe," he told his fresh claro as he stopped in a dark doorway to light it, "the guys we just saw are after somebody else? San Jose is full of foreign consulates, spies, soldiers of fortune, and stuff. Is there any law saying we're the *only* guys anyone could be after? Shit, we're not even wanted by the Costa Rican cops, bless their little hearts."

The claro had no sensible answers to offer. So he just smoked it as he made his way back to the hotel. He checked his pocket watch near the rear entrance. It was almost a quarter to three. Whatever they did, they had to get out of the hotel poco tiempo. It was probably safe enough to make a run for that other posada Gaston knew about. Latins tended to be night people, but at this hour even the streets of San Jose were pretty deserted.

He slipped in the back way unobserved. That had been the general idea. He moved up the stairwell, hoping by now Gaston and the princess were through screwing and that she didn't have much luggage to worry about.

The hall carpets were lush, and the big American moved light-footed in any case. So as he rounded the corner leading to Room 207, the two guys facing said door had their backs to him.

Captain Gringo suppressed a startled gasp and drew his .38 instead as he took in the scene in one horrified glance. The intent of the two burly guys in native dress was all too obvious. One already had the lit bomb in his hand in motion as the other kicked Princess Manukai's door in for him to *throw* it!

Captain Gringo moved fast for a man his size, as many a slower man had learned the hard way. But it seemed as if time were standing still and that he were hauling his gun hand and gun through air thicker than glue. He watched the bomb float in slow motion into the darkness of 207 like a bubble and then—too late, he realized sickly—the .38 in his numb right hand was firing with the maddening slowness of a steeple bell sounding the death knell.

To the men he was gunning, it seemed a lot faster, of course. Both stood dead in their tracks before they knew they were dead or had time to fall. For, in truth, Captain Gringo got off five pistol rounds that sounded more like a burst of automatic fire. Then the doorway of Room 207 lit up bright orange, and Captain Gringo was knocked on his ass by the shock wave of the explosion!

Cursing, trying not to puke, the heartsick American rolled around the corner and sprang to his feet, instinctively heading for cover while up and down the corridor people blasted awake began to shout all at once.

But before anyone could open an embarrassing door, Captain Gringo made it to his own suite and ducked inside, thanking God Gaston hadn't thought to lock it after fixing it—and cursing God for what had just happened to Gaston and a great lay as well!

For a long, sick moment he braced his back in the dark against the door he'd just slammed shut against the whole cruel world. He knew he had a few minutes, maybe more, to think. He just couldn't think *straight* at the moment. He'd lost the only friend he trusted south of the Rio Grande, and with the princess blown away as well, there was no point in running for Puntarenas, so . . . Okay, where was he supposed to run?

It was a good question. He wanted to take a thoughtful drag on his claro while considering the matter, saw he'd left it somewhere in his recent travels, and fished out another to light up. As he struck a match he blinked and gasped, "What the fuck?" and then flipped the light switch. Because the couple in his bed had not only messed it up a lot, fucking in it, but had either managed to kill themselves or at least knock themselves out in the process!

Captain Gringo laughed like an idiot who'd just been pardoned the night before his scheduled execution as he moved over to the bed where Gaston lay in the arms of Morpheus as well as Princess Manukai. As he bent over to shake the little Frenchman, he inhaled the rising fumes, nodded, and said, "Yeah, she said she was out of booze. But I used to have Jamaica as well as gin in here. Wake up, you sex-mad drunk. We got troubles."

Gaston opened one bleary eye and mumbled, "Don't hit me, Dick. I know you saw her first, but she overpowered me."

"I believe you. That's not the problem. Didn't you hear all that noise just now?"

"There was noise, my jealous lover? Tell me about it in the morning."

"Goddamn it, it *is* morning, and they hit sooner than we expected them to! They just gave the princess here a dandy excuse for that busted bed. They tossed a *bomb* in it! That's one down and two to go. So cut the comedy and help me fort up!"

Without waiting for an answer, he moved back to the door and proceeded to reload his .38 as Gaston swung his naked feet to the floor, sat up, and rubbed his face, groaning, "Merde alors, I feel sick."

Captain Gringo growled, "It must have been someone you ate. Heads up. I hear the pitter-patter of little feet coming our way!"

He switched off the overhead light just as someone pounded on the door authoritatively and a voice called out, "Hotel Security! Is anyone in there?"

Captain Gringo held the .38 politely out of sight as he cracked the door to reply innocently, "My pal just went to get some more liquor. We're, ah, having a party. What's up?"

The hotel dick, with an anxious night clerk standing behind him, said, "Oh, it is you, Señor Walker? Forgive me, we do not wish for to be officious, but we just had a terrible thing happen on this floor and wish for to make certain our other guests are all right!"

"I heard what sounded like an explosion just now," replied Captain Gringo, trying not to sound too interested as he added, "What happened?"

The house dick made the sign of the cross and said, "In God's truth, I wish we knew! You cannot see it from here, but just around the far corner two pobrecitos lie dead on the rug. They must have been killed by their own bomb. It is only just, no?"

"They had a bomb?"

"Si, more than one. Two others lie between them in the corridor. I have told no one to touch either until La Policia arrive. It looks as if they meant to throw all three into the suite of the poor Princess Manukai. But the first one was more powerful than they thought, and now at least the state is saved the expense of a trial!"

Captain Gringo said that sounded fair as well as logical. Then, willing to press his luck a bit for more information, he asked, "Princess, you say, Señor? Is she all right?"

The house dick answered, "Si, some kind of South Sea Island royalty. You must have seen her around the hotel. A great brown woman. The bomb was most obviously intended for her as some sort of political assassination. But God smiled on us all. She was not in her suite at the time. In fact, she seems to have left the hotel. There is no baggage in her suite. I certainly *hope* she's gone for good. We don't really want such exciting guests in this hotel. We're never going to get all that blood out of the hall carpeting; and as for what they did to suite two-oh-seven, Madre de Dios!"

Captain Gringo nodded knowingly and reached in his pants as he said, "Some people just don't deserve such sophisticated surroundings. They don't understand that they're not supposed to make noise after midnight."

He handed out enough to make them both feel very happy as he added, "We wouldn't have started our own quiet little party had we known the place was about to blow up and attract the attention of La Policia. But we'll get the whores out of here as soon as my friend gets back, eh?"

The house dick and room clerk exchanged glances as well as the tip. The house dick put a finger to the side of his nose, winked, and said, "We did not hear that, Señor. If we had, I would have to chide you for being naughty. But since we did not and La Policia will be here any minute, the last thing the management wishes for to explain is wicked women whose names do not appear on the pages downstairs!''

"Look, we don't want the girls picked up either. But won't the cops want to question everyone on this floor?"

"For why, Señor? Did not Pepe here and me just see you and your friend come in alone after the explosion?"

The night clerk cleared his throat nervously and asked the older and more cynical house dick, "What if El Señor's friend comes in from the bodega after we have just told La Policia he is in his suite?" So the house dick snorted in disgust and said, "Estupido, he went out again for to get some medication for his nerves after learning of the attempted assassination on his floor, of course! Leave it to me. I am the one they will be talking to, no? Come, let us see to the other guests.''

He winked again at Captain Gringo and they moved on, the house dick still explaining how a good house dick kept the cops out of the hair of innocent guests. Captain Gringo closed the door, locked it, and switched on the light again.

The scene across the room hadn't changed, save that Gaston was enjoying a healthy belt of Jamaica as Princess Manukai went on dreaming with a contented Mona Lisa smile. Captain Gringo growled, "Okay, you heard all that. So now you know more than *I* do! What the fuck were you two doing in my bed when they hit earlier than expected?"

Gaston replied, "Fucking, of course. Her bed was ruined even before they blew it up, and this one was closer than mine as we dashed gaily down the corridor. Have you ever dashed a six-foot-six naked woman gaily down a corridor, Dick? If you ever do, I assure you that you will feel speed is of the essence!"

"Oh great! Didn't you even bring her kimono?"

Gaston stood up, tottered around to the other side of the bed, and—staring down at things Captain Gringo couldn't see from his side—said, "Oui, there it is, under my hat. I scooped up as much as I could before she could drag me out the door by the dong. Have you noticed what a très impulsive child the adorable little thing is? She seems to want what she wants when she wants it. So when I pointed out the disadvantages of an already collapsed bed and suggested mine—"

"Never mind the details," Captain Gringo cut in, adding with a grim smile: "Sometimes it pays to be impulsive. But I sure wish you'd taken time to move her luggage as well as her ass. The hotel help just said there isn't any in her room right now."

"I heard. Perhaps her belongings were blown out the window? Never underestimate what a freak explosion may do, hein?"

Captain Gringo shrugged and said, "Never underestimate the resident sneak thieves you'll find in most hotels, either. Either way, we're stuck with one big broad who doesn't own a thing at the moment but a kimono at least two sizes too small for her, and we have to sneak her out of here before sunrise!"

Gaston sat down beside her again, glass in one hand, as with the other he gently raised one of her eyelids, nodded to himself, and said, "You forgot to add 'unconscious.' If she wasn't so formidable, she'd be dead as well. She drinks like a species of fish, and while we are on the subject, you must have noticed she's a rather simpleminded species of slut, hein?"

"Hey, let's be fair, you horny old goat. We both fucked her, and she didn't ask either of us for money. Where in the South Sea Constitution does it say a guy who lays two dames in one night is a sportsman while a dame who lays two guys is a slut?"

Gaston sighed and replied, "Eh bien, I deserved that. But my remark was more concerned with her *brains* than her *morals*. Aside from being an easy lay, our adorable princess has broken every rule in the skulduggerist's survival manual. She has blabbed her already risky plan all over a très tough town; and as we just observed, people we don't even know are not at all enthused about them. There is no way on earth we could board the coast train with an almost naked giant lady without attracting attention and . . ."

"I forgot to tell you," Captain Gringo cut in. "Some *other* guys who don't seem to want those natives rescued have the depot staked out. So we couldn't smuggle her aboard *any* train, dressed as a nun!"

"Merde alors, that tears it, then. I know you are going to say this sounds . . . how you say, chickenshit, but has it occurred to you that they are after *her*, not *us*, at the moment?"

Captain Gringo said, "When you're right, you're right. It sounds chickenshit, even coming from you, you old fart!"

Gaston finished his drink and rose again, walking around to gather up his clothing as he insisted, "Did I ever tell you how one gets to *be* an old fart? For one thing, one starts by not getting killed while one is a *young* fart! Let us consider the matter from a practique point of view instead of the passion we both feel for this sleeping beauty, Dick. We were not the ones who kidnapped her adorable pearl-diving peones. We were not the ones who advised her to go to the German consulate to make rude remarks about a German-owned company and then tell all the street people of San Jose what she intended to do about the grotesque situation. We just saved her life once, gratis. So she's one life, countless orgasms, and almost all our booze *ahead* of us! Didn't your mother ever tell you how wise it is to run for the lifeboats while the doomed ship was still afloat?"

Captain Gringo shook his head and said, "It's the rats, not the men, who desert the sinking ship. You're right about her being too dumb to be let out without a leash. So we can't just leave her here. We'll have to get her dressed and over to that other hideout, poco tiempo. We're never going to make it after sunrise, and we're running out of night by the minute!''

Gaston went on bitching and dressing as Captain Gringo moved to the window, looked out, and said, ''Bueno, I see the roof of the shop next door comes to just under the second-story sills on this side.''

Gaston just cursed in a mixture of French, Spanish, and Arabic. So Captain Gringo only understood two-thirds of the dumb things he was supposed to be. He nodded and said, ''Okay, Don Quixote was an asshole too, but this windmill says she's willing to pay a thousand a week and screws pretty good as well.''

''Merde alors, who said anything about lasting a week in her company? We've known her less than twelve hours, and all sorts of people we don't even know are out to kill us!''

Captain Gringo moved over to the bed, saying, ''Like you said before, I think it's her they're after. Hand me that kimono.''

Gaston did, saying, ''Have you considered this is all the poor child owns in the world right now? How is she supposed to *pay* us if someone stole her luggage, clothing, and purse, hein?''

''Will you stop trying to cross bridges we haven't even seen yet?'' the tall American replied, bending over to shake the Kanaka girl's big brown shoulder, saying, ''Rise and shine, Doll. We gotta move it down the road.''

Manukai fluttered her eyes, sighed contentedly, and purred, ''Whose turn is it to make nukinuki with me?''

He grimaced, shook her harder, and insisted, ''Hey, no shit, wake up. We have to haul ass out of here. The cold gray dawn is on its way, and judging by the noise outside, the cops are already here!''

That did it. She suddenly sat up, blinking in confusion, and asked what was going on. He explained as much as her still-befuddled mind could grasp while he helped her into her kimono, tried to fasten it more modestly over her big brown tits, and discovered it was, yeah, at least two sizes too small for her. But there was nothing anyone could do about that now. So he told Gaston, "Don't just stand there, damn it. Hit the light switch and help me get her out the goddam window!"

Gaston did. But once they were supporting the big wobbly-legged Kanaka girl between them on the tar-paper roof next door, Gaston pointed out that dropping her over the edge into the alley seemed as rude as just tossing her out a second-story window in the first place.

Captain Gringo said, "Make for that roof hatch near the chimney, you jerk-off. There has to be a ladder or a flight of steps leading down inside the shop, right?"

Gaston helped him get the princess over to it and dropped to one knee to get out his all-purpose pocketknife, but even as he made short work of the lock, whispered, "What if someone lives over the shop?"

"Asshole, if I didn't know this was a one-story building with no quarters in the back, we wouldn't be *doing* this! But get your thirty-eight out anyway. *I* could be an asshole, too."

He wasn't. Once they'd popped the roof hatch and manhandled the big girl down the steep steps, they found themselves in the flower shop catering mostly to guests in the hotel next door; and, naturally, nobody was about to buy a bouquet at this hour. As he left Manukai in Gaston's charge to scout the back exit, the princess helped herself to a big red rose for her long black hair, explaining with a sigh that a hibiscus blossom would really be more fashionable where she came from.

The back door and alleyway seemed clear. So the two

soldiers of fortune braced the princess between them and
started making tracks as she kept staggering and saying,
"Wheeeee!"

Gaston said, "This is not going to work, Dick. The
no-questions posada I mentioned is just too far for this
toddler to toddle, hein?"

"Okay, what's closer? You're supposed to know this
town like the back of your hand, right?"

"Oui, but there is nothing on the back of my hand, less
than ten blocks away, except the home of a certain widow I
occasionally visit when I am truly desperate."

"Do you think she'll take us in?"

"Sacre Bleu, she'd take in Jack the Ripper, even if she
knew it was him! But at least one of us would have to
repay her hospitality with a good screwing, and for some
reason, a scrawny old woman with a mustache simply fails
to appeal to me at the moment!"

"You'd rather spend the next few nights of your life in
jail? Get us to cover poco tiempo, you maniac!"

"Listen to him, Mon Dieu, he calls *me* a maniac as we
stagger down the street with a crazy lady with a rose in her
hair between us! Mais very well, swing right at the next
corner. You're going to have to service our petite and
antique hostess, though. I couldn't get it up again tonight
with a block and tackle!"

The Creole widow they awoke from her beauty rest
wasn't quite as ugly as Captain Gringo had expected,
having heard Gaston's bitching description of her for the
last three blocks and an alleyway. One could see, as she
came to the back door in her thin nightgown, that she
hadn't been built too bad, say thirty years ago. Her

mustache wasn't that thick; her long gray hair framed a face that, while wrinkled a bit, still had nice bone structure. Her *brains* left a lot to be desired, though. She hauled them in and bolted her back door behind them before Gaston had finished explaining what the hell he was doing there with two total strangers at this hour.

Her name was Felicia. She seemed more interested in Manukai than in either soldier of fortune, but if she had lesbian leanings, they didn't show as she shot daggers of suspicion at the younger and even less modestly dressed Kanaka girl. But when Gaston explained the poor thing was suffering from shock after almost being assassinated, old Felicia helped them get her to a guest room. So all might have turned out well had not Manukai, suffering from the early stages of sobriety and the rose in her hair, hung on to Gaston as they got her into bed. Captain Gringo told her to let go, adding, "You're with me. Felicia here is Gaston's date."

But the willful, and powerful, princess giggled girlishly and hauled poor Gaston down against her, insisting, "Bullshit, I want some more French loving, and this sweet little thing eats pussy better than anyone I've ever met!"

The older woman gasped, "Oh!" as if she'd been slapped. Captain Gringo took her by one arm and moved her back out into the hall, explaining soothingly, "She's out of her head. She doesn't know what she's saying. You're still Gaston's girl, Felicia."

The older Creole woman sobbed. "You are most gallant, Señor Deek. But I know all too well what I am to any man these days. It has been a long time since I have been anything but a how-you-say port in the storm, even for older men. That big mestiza is most attractive, once one recovers from the first surprise, no?"

They both could now hear bedsprings groaning inside. He led her farther away, saying, "She's some sort of crazy

South Sea Islander, not a mestiza. Don't blame Gaston. I
don't think he has much say in the matter; and, frankly, we
have to keep her happy as well as safe right now. Come
on. I'll explain the whole setup to you.''

He expected her to lead him to her kitchen. He felt more
resigned than surprised when they wound up in another
bedroom instead. Old Felicia sat him beside her on the bed
she'd no doubt just woke up in—lonely as hell—and said,
''I'm listening, but this had better be good. Gaston and me
are old, ah, friends. But really, to bring another woman to
my house and do wicked things to her right under my
nose!''

He took her hand and patted it as he gave her a short
and not completely truthful rundown of the situation.
When he got to the part about them both working for the
princess for big money, Felicia sighed and said, ''I might
have known Gaston was after her *money* as well! I am sure
that if our Gaston had been born a woman, he would have
been a most rich whore by this time!''

Captain Gringo chuckled and said, ''No bet. I see we've
both known him a while, Felicia. Funny, he never mentioned
you to me before, though.''

She shrugged, gave a defeated little sigh, and asked,
''Why should he have mentioned me to anyone? It's not as
if I'm a conquest for any man to boast of, and, in truth,
he's only made love to me . . . let me see, seven times,
spread out over almost as many years, of course.''

''Good lord, do you keep score, Felicia?''

''*You* will too, when you reach my age. While my late
husband still lived, I was used to making love almost
every night for many years, although it now seems such a
short time I was young and beautiful. Now I count the rare
occasions when some man who can find nothing better is
willing to settle for an old sack of bones like me. It has
been . . . exactly six months and twelve nights since I last

made love, if that is what one wishes to call a fat drunk locked out of his own house by a fat wife.''

He stared soberly down at her in the dim candlelight of her lonely room and almost meant it when he assured her, ''Come on, you're not a bad-looking woman, Felicia.''

It was her turn to pat his hand as she said bitterly, ''You don't have to be kind to your grandmother, you sweet child. She looks in the mirror every time she combs her hair, and when she looks, she curses God and asks him why he treated her this way!''

She lowered her gray head sadly to stare dully at the tile floor as she added, almost to herself, in a hurt, puzzled tone, ''What did I do to deserve such punishment? I was a faithful wife, a good mother until my only sweet little niño died of the vomito negro. Before the saints treated me so cruelly, I lit candles to all of them, every feast day. Now I never go to church, and I sin every chance I get, for in God's truth, one gets little chance to sin *these* days!''

He answered, softly as well as awkwardly, ''Well, everybody has to get older if they live long enough, right?''

She said, ''Just you wait and see how quickly it sneaks up on you! I am not as bitter about the years running through my fingers like grains of sand as I am the *emptiness* of each long night. I always knew I would be old some day. I did not know I would still feel passion. Why do I still feel passion now that I am so old and withered, on the outside at least?''

''Maybe you're just healthy?''

She heaved a vast sigh and said, ''I fear I may be. It's a funny thing. But as we get older, we fail to *feel* older. Old is always twenty years in the *future,* never where we *are*!''

He frowned thoughtfully, trying to understand. She knew he didn't. So she explained, ''When one is twenty, forty sounds old. But by the time one reaches thirty, forty does not sound really old. At thirty, one is sure that *fifty* is when one will start feeling old; but then, by the time one is forty, *sixty* seems a more reasonable date for the beginning of one's old age; and yet, when one reaches fifty—''

He cut in. ''I follow you,'' he said, not wanting to know just how old she really was. What he wanted right now was a graceful exit from this confusing conversation. The night was shot. He still hadn't gotten any sleep. It seemed like a good idea to get some. She was obviously up for the day. So how did you ask a lady in a nightie to show you to bed? He decided the direct approach was as good as anything else he could come up with. So he yawned and said, ''I have to get the princess some duds and dinero by noon, at least. I know we're imposing on you a lot, Felicia, but I sure could use some shut-eye.''

She sighed and said, ''Of course. I have but one guest room. Our Gaston and that big brown pig are abusing my hospitality indeed in it. But if you wish for to stretch out here, I assure you I will not attack you in your sleep.''

He chuckled and said, ''Oh, that wouldn't bother me at all.''

He'd meant it as innocent gallantry. He realized he shouldn't have said a thing like that to a sex-starved widow when Felicia gasped, ''Oh, por favor, God, make him *mean* that!'' while, suiting actions to prayer, she proceeded to shuck her nightgown over her gray head!

He gulped in dismay as she exposed her somewhat withered charms by candlelight. Then, either because the candlelight was kinder by far than Mr. Edison, or perhaps because of the contrast between her petite white body and the last one he'd been paying any attention to, he began to wonder what on earth he was *dismayed* about!

She seemed to be gray-haired all over. But other than that, Felicia was built like a sixteen-year-old. So he took her into his arms and kissed her as they fell back together across the mattress. He couldn't tell, as she kissed back desperately, whether she still had all her teeth or a damned fine set of dentures. It didn't seem to matter, if a guy kept his eyes shut and just went on kissing while they both got *his* clothes out of the way. But he had to rise above her to get into position to do anything more important; and as he did so, Felicia covered her face with her hands and said, "Oh, don't look at me! Don't spoil the magic, Deek!"

So he didn't. He rolled up and out to snuff the candle. Then, in the merciful darkness, he found a once-more young and beautiful girl waiting for him, trembling with desire, and as he entered her, he didn't have to feel so noble after all. He'd always thought dirty old women were supposed to have dried-up prunes or something between their thighs. This one had the moist, pulsating vagina of a passionate, maybe thirty-year-old, woman of adventurous tastes. Her thighs felt great too, as she locked her legs around his bare waist, gasping, "Oh, Jesus, Maria y Jose, if heaven feels any better than this, let me die right now!"

He had to admit she had a point as he got down to serious business in her sweet old business. Thanks to earlier excitement, the sharp edge of his virility had been dulled. But keeping it up in such pleasant surroundings didn't seem to be as big a problem as he'd thought it might be when Gaston first suggested this crazy notion. Poor old Felicia came almost at once, moaning in pent-up ecstasy, and since he of course was still getting used to this unplanned if not obscene adventure, he naturally just kept humping away as she came down from the stars in a series of contented contractions, gasping, "You wish *more*? I can't believe it! Most men, once they have had their way with me . . ."

He said, "Shut up about other men, Querida. This is a private orgy we're having, right?"

She giggled in a surprisingly girlish way. Apparently the

knack never left one, in bed at least, so she giggled again and said, "Es verdad, you are not like other men at all, Querido. But are you sure you are not just being kind to an old woman out of respect for her age?"

He laughed and thrust harder in her as he asked, "Does this feel like respect?" And she moaned, "Oh, Cristo, no! It feels like cock, a big one! Faster, faster, I am coming againnnnnnn!"

She sure was, and the hell of it was, he *couldn't*. He knew it wasn't her fault. In the dark, old Felicia was yummy enough to make a guy come in her fast. Or she would have been if he hadn't just been raped by a sex-mad Kanaka. But at least the princess had done all the work. So while his shaft was sort of weary, his back and wind were still in good enough shape to keep going and, what the hell, there was no telling *when* this poor old broad was going to get laid *again*.

She sure seemed to be enjoying this one as she moved her smaller body in time with his thrusts, panting, "I am so happy and so grateful, Deek!"

He said, "Don't talk silly. You're fantastic in bed and you know it."

"Oh god, do you really like for to make love to me, Deek? You are not just being kind?"

He was, sort of, now that he was starting to sweat and it was starting to look as though he just weren't meant to ever come again. But he made himself pound harder as he replied, "Hell, if I wasn't kind, I'd really hurt you. It's all I can do to keep from letting myself go really crazy in you."

"Oh, please *do!* I wish for you to possess me most completely, my lovely young bull! Do not hold back, Deek! Pound me! Hurt me! Make me feel like a frightened virgin again!"

Now, that sounded a little silly, even with the candle

snuffed; but now that he'd gotten himself into this dumb situation, the only polite way out seemed to be some macho bullshit, even if he had to fake it. So he growled deep in his throat, kissed her roughly to keep her from saying something that might make him laugh at the wrong time, and moved in and out of her wildly before the stupid, tired dong could go soft in there until, as he knew it was about to, he collapsed weakly on her, gasping, "Jeeee-zuss!" in English. He'd found Latin dames found English groaning as exotic as Yankee gals found the rumbling of Latin lovers. She held him tightly to her little chest, asking gently, "Did I satisfy you, Querido?"

He chuckled and said, "No. I always fake it. Couldn't you tell?"

It worked. She giggled and replied, "The only thing to be said for the state my hair is in these days is that I don't have to worry about all that sweet love liquid you have filled me to the brim with. Oh, it's running out of me now, and it feels so friendly!"

He didn't answer. He hadn't come once in her. But she was sort of juicy now. It did feel friendly. So he saw no reason to withdraw. He knew he'd never get it back in now if he did.

Felicia took that as a compliment, too. She crooned, "Oh, you feel so nice, just snuggled up inside me like that. Could we just lie like this for a time? I know you will come to your senses any moment, but let me feel like a woman a little longer, por favor?"

That sounded fair. In fact, as he got his second wind, it felt pretty good. So he started moving in her again, in slow, teasing thrusts. She began to move the same way, but asked, "Is this possible, Deek?"

He said, "Probably not. But it doesn't hurt. Doesn't hurt me, at least. Am I getting heavy for you?" And she said, "Si, I *love* it!" as she began to move faster, asking, "Maybe if I got on top?"

It would have been a good idea if he'd really intended to come in her at this late date. But though he wanted to, he knew he couldn't, so why make a big deal out of it? He said, "Just take it easy, and let's see what happens. A man doesn't need acrobatics with a muchacha as sweet as you."

She sobbed. "Oh, what a nice thing to say!" she managed, and started crying in his arms as he kissed her soothingly, comforting her with polite, faked passion until, all of a sudden, it felt real enough and, yeah, if he really pounded harder, before the treacherous little bastard could poop out on him again . . .

"Madre de Dios!" gasped Felicia as he started to let himself go, not worrying about his performance now that he had a good excuse for failing to ejaculate. So, of course, he came in her, in a long, shuddering orgasm she shared with a surprised scream of sheer animal lust.

That did it, for him at least. When she shyly suggested they try and get some sleep, he wasn't about to argue. He rolled off to flop across the mattress spread-eagle, and to hell with where the pillows were. Felicia hesitated before she asked him shyly, "Would it distress you if I lay my head upon your big strong shoulder, Deek?"

He said it sounded like a hell of a good idea. So, as he dozed off, the sweet old broad snuggled against him like the shy bride she must have been before he was born; and when he thought about it, that old fairy tale about Sir Gawain and Lady Greensleeves was a crock of shit. Old Gawain may have taken credit for more sacrifice than he'd really felt when he agreed to marry that old crone for King Arthur. If Lady Greensleeves had been half as good in the dark as good old Felicia, the slob hadn't suffered all that much.

• • •

Felicia must have been telling the truth about not getting much excitement these days. For when Captain Gringo woke up to see sunlight streaming through the shutter slats of her bedroom, she was still fast asleep. He eased out of bed to avoid waking her. He tried not to look at her as he quickly dressed. Sir Gawain had probably been anxious to put on his armor and go fight a dragon everytime he woke up with Lady Greensleeves or, wait, it hadn't been that bad in the fairy tale. Old Greensleeves had been a nice-looking young broad in the *daytime*. Those fucking knights got *all* the breaks.

He didn't look in on Gaston and the princess. He knew what they both looked like with their duds off, and he didn't want to wrestle with another dame in the foreseeable future.

As he let himself out of Felicia's house and got his bearings he told himself he probably should have gotten Princess Manukai's permission for what he was hoping to get away with. But, what the hell, it was probably illegal anyway, and it wasn't as if he were out to *rob* the big dumb broad.

He saw it was later than he'd thought, damn it. The tropic sun was frying any eggs anyone might be dumb enough to leave on the sidewalks of San Jose; and if he didn't hurry, the office would be closing for La Siesta and another day would be about shot.

He'd have to forgo the steam bath he'd intended before approaching good old Olivia at International Express. He'd wiped himself clean on Felicia's sheets before sneaking out of her bed. But one never knew how one's own body might smell to others. So on the way to the main drag, he stopped to pick up some bay rum, ducked into a public latrine, and doused himself where it might matter most. The bay rum burned his balls like hell. But at least they might smell as though they'd just enjoyed a hot shave instead of two hot women in a row.

He made it to the big bronze doors of International Express just as they were about to get locked and stay that way until at least three. There were no other customers inside. Olivia Ascot, the English dame that really ran the joint no matter what the office letterheads might say, invited him into her private office, saying, "Long time no see, Dick. What can I do for you, assuming you're here on business, you mean old thing."

He laughed lightly and took a seat by her desk, fishing out a claro as she sat down behind it and tried to look imposing. If there was one thing Olivia Ascot didn't look, it was imposing. Snooty, perhaps. The ash-blond London lady had long since given up her Proper Cockney accent in favor of one more suited to a Mayfair shop girl—in a shop the queen bought her hats in.

Since they were in the tropics instead of Mayfair, however, she was dressed more like a Gibson girl planning to play tennis during La Siesta. He wondered if she knew her bodice wasn't properly buttoned. When a lady had chest measurements like that, it was probably tough to keep all the buttons from popping open.

He lit the claro without asking permission, since they were old friends indeed, and said, "Just got back from losing a revolution in Nicaragua. Have you ever heard of the Princess Manukai of Konakona?"

"Liar." Olivia sighed, adding, "You've been back in San Jose for *weeks* and you've never come to see me *once*!"

He nodded and said, "I was afraid to. I'm involved in some of my usual work, and this time with people who play rough. Last night they robbed the princess of all her cash, passport, and so forth. So, I repeat, have you ever heard of her, Doll?"

Olivia rose and moved over to a bank of filing cabinets, offering him a nice rear view as she asked, "How do you spell that weird name again?"

He spelled "Manukai" and "Konakona" for her, wondering how the hell a dame wearing white linen from the nape of her neck down to her trim ankles could look so naked. It was probably because he remembered. He'd forgotten how yummy the back of her neck looked with her blond hair pinned up like that. She slid open a drawer, rummaged about in it, and said, "You're in luck, Dick. She has an account with us."

He said, "I figured she might," as Olivia resumed her seat, facing him, and spread the financial dossier on the green blotter between them. She asked, "What do you want to know about her? If she's ever stiffed a shop for a box of candy, it'll be in here."

He said, "I already figured her credit would be good. Her old man's a cannibal king or something. Here's the problem, Honey. We have to get her down to Puntarenas and, at the moment, she hasn't got a wooden nickel to work with. Can do?"

The English girl said, "I'll have to see," as she began to go over the big Kanaka girl's credit rating, reading half aloud, "Manukai, Princess. That's her title, not her first name. Apparently they don't have more than one name and, yes, she's the oldest daughter and co-heir of his current majesty, King Kamamamoku of Konakona. Perishing wog probably rules a kingdom no bigger than Hyde Park but, I say, he *does* have a triple-A credit rating. Missionaries must have taught him to pay his bills, what?"

"The princess said her people were sort of advanced. What about *her* credit rating?"

Olivia's voice sounded a little grudging as she replied,

"Same thing. Bloody unlimited credit. She could buy a yacht on her signature alone, as far as we're concerned. Oh, it says here she graduated from Vassar eighteen months ago. Pity. If all the Vassar girls were laid end to end . . ."

"I wouldn't be surprised," Captain Gringo finished for her, adding: "You keep forgetting I'm a New Englander. But leaving her choice of mainland schools aside, she's already got a yacht. So we just need enough to get her a new outfit and get her down to it in Puntarenas. So how's about it, Doll Box?"

"You just leave my box out of this until I decide whether I'm still cross with you, Dick Walker! As for your precious princess, certainly. All she has to do is come in to sign a bank draft, and we'll give her all the money she can carry. Sometimes I wish *I* were royal."

He chuckled and said, "You're prettier than the Princess of Wales. Uh, couldn't you just give me, say, five hundred U.S. in her name, Olivia?"

The English girl frowned at him and said, "Don't be silly. Do you look like a South Sea Island princess? By the way, what *does* this perishing princess of yours look like, Dick? I already know I'm better-looking than the Princess of *Wales*."

That wasn't quite true, if the pictures he'd seen of fat Prince Teddy's beautiful Danish wife hadn't been retouched at least a little. But he let that pass and just said, "For one thing, Princess Manukai is about six-foot-six and has to weigh at least two hundred. Let's get back to her financial problems. It's not like I'm asking for a *lot,* you know."

Olivia sighed and said, "Dick, I don't see why I have to explain all this to a big boy like you, but I'm not supposed to release *any* of her money to anyone but *her,* and even *she's* supposed to *sign* for it! So just bring the perishing great wog in, let her make at least an X for me, and I'll be glad to give you all the money she needs!''

He shook his head and said, "Can't. You see, at the moment she's holed up across town without a stitch of clothing or . . . okay, a kimono and no shoes.''

"You . . . bastard!'' Olivia flared, her voice dripping venom as she added: "I might have known any woman you were involved with would have to be naked! Of all the perishing nerve! To come in here and ask me to give you money, illegally, for another bloody woman!''

"Now don't get your bowels in an uproar, Doll,'' he soothed, going on to explain: "I wasn't the one who stole her things. Someone tried to assassinate her with a bomb last night, and she lost everything she had in the explosion!''

Olivia calmed down enough to say, "I think I read something about that in *La Prenza* this morning. Didn't make the connection. So, all right, where was she, and where were *you*, when someone blew all her clothes off?''

He grinned and said, "You'd never believe me.'' And she said, grimly, "Try me.'' So he said, meeting her narrow gaze with an innocent smile, "I was over at the railroad depot when the assassins snuck in. The reason they didn't blow her up was that she was in bed with my pal, Gaston, at the time. You remember Gaston, don't you?''

She laughed incredulously and said, "I certainly do, and you say she's six-foot-six?''

"What can I tell you? Some guys like a little meat with their potatoes.''

She laughed louder despite herself, and said, "The picture is too funny for words, even though I should be ashamed of myself for picturing anything so wild! But you're just making the whole thing up, aren't you? I mean, honestly, Dick, do you expect me to buy little Gaston as a giant-Vassar-girl-in-blackface's lover?''

Captain Gringo shrugged and said, "What do you want, my word as an officer and gentleman?"

She sobered and said, "You're hardly a gentleman. But I do know you take your word as an officer seriously. So, all right, it's ridiculous but I believe you. It's too wild a story for even you to make up."

"Bueno. Just give me about five hundred, and I'll sign for it."

"Oh God, here we go again. How on earth do *you* intend to sign for anything from International Express, Dick? I don't know how to tell you this, but as a wanted man with a price on your head, your credit rating really isn't all that grand."

He said, "All I need is a pen and a paper to sign, damn it. I told you I knew how to spell 'Manukai,' and 'princess' starts with a 'p,' doesn't it?"

She gasped. "Jesus Christ, I know I sucked you off that time I got sort of carried away, Dick! But do you seriously expect me to be party to a *forgery*!"

"Picky picky picky, what's a little penmanship between old pals? I give you my word—and you know it's good— that I'm not trying to steal any of your firm's petty cash."

"No, you're trying to get *me* to steal it *for* you! I could lose my bloody job! I could even go to prison!"

"How? Who's going to know? The office is closed. So where are any witnesses to say it was me instead of a shy Island maiden who signed for the dough? You have her signature on file, don't you?"

"Of course. But it would still be forgery if I let you copy it, Dick!"

"So don't let me. Just give me the damned form and a copy of her official signature and then go get a drink of water or something. We both know nobody will ever examine it unless someone raises a question about its being genuine, and who's going to bitch—the princess? She *wants* the damned money. She can't go home without it!"

Olivia still hesitated, so he insisted. "No shit, Doll Box, I wouldn't ask if it wasn't really important as hell to me."

She hesitated again, then sighed and said, "Oh damn, you're going to ruin me, but you know I just never have been able to resist you."

She reached in a drawer, handed him the proper form and some scrap to practice on, then turned the dossier around to give him a clear view of the big Kanaka girl's official signature as she rose, saying, "I'm going in for a smoke in the lounge next door. Naturally, if you can get to the princess and back before I finish, oh, a couple of cigarettes, I'll have no way of knowing anything but the fact you produced a properly made-out draft. So I naturally had to give you the money, right?"

He told her she was a swell kid. She said she was a perishing chump and left him alone with her desk at his entire disposal. He got right to work.

Captain Gringo was hardly a professional forger. But he'd learned military sketching as well as mapmaking at the Point, and the signature was pretty simple. Princess Manukai wrote more like a little girl than a princess might be expected to. He'd suspected the veneer of western culture her folks had bought her was a little thin. He screwed up his first attempt, got it right on the second, and then signed the bond paper pretty well, in all modesty. He saw the rest of the form was blank. Olivia still had to fill in the date, amount, and so forth before she could give him the cash. That would be no problem, with the office deserted for at least another three hours or more. He really didn't want to get the kid in trouble, and the fact that nobody would ever be able to say whether she'd given the money to him or the Czar Of All The Russias might help keep her out of any.

He knew his way into the lounge. Old Olivia had entertained him during La Siesta before, as he remembered fondly. As he came through the doorway with the papers in hand, he saw she seemed to want to entertain him there again, unless she always smoked bare-ass, reclining on a leather couch.

As she looked up at him languorously, he said, "I guess you don't want to open the safe right now, huh?"

Olivia opened her creamy white thighs instead as she purred, "Screw the safe for now. Better yet, get over here and screw me *right*, you bad boy! Mamma wants to make sure you haven't been bad with other little girls, and there's only one way to find out. So if you can't get it *up*, get *out*!"

He laughed, not sure he meant it, as he considered all the sacrifices he'd been called on to make lately, just to keep that crazy big Kanaka broad out of more serious trouble.

But, somehow, once he was going at it hot and heavy with the beautiful ash-blonde on the nice firm couch, his labor in Princess Manukai's behalf seemed worth the effort.

It was a dark and foggy dawn when they arrived at the seaport of Puntarenas after an all-night run by private coach. They paid off the shady coachman and shotgun messenger Gaston had recruited from among the rogues of San Jose and sent them on their way. When Gaston said the discreet posada they'd be checking into was only five blocks away, the princess asked how come. Captain Gringo took her arm and explained, "If anyone ever asks those hombres where they dropped us off, we don't want them handing out our exact address, see?" He didn't add that moving cross-country with a giant Kanaka, unobserved, had been enough of a bitch. It wasn't Manukai's fault that, even wearing her new Costa Rican campesina costume, with her long hair braided mestiza style, she didn't make a very convincing second-class citizen of any Central American country *he'd* ever been through. He told her to remember she was a cheap pickup in case they passed anyone on the streets at this hour as Gaston took her other arm and said, "Eh bien, this way, my children. Thank god we don't have any other baggage to worry about."

Manukai giggled and asked, "Which one of you sailors am I supposed to be with, or did we settle on group rates?"

Captain Gringo laughed, but asked, "Don't you ever think of anything but sex, Princess?" And she replied, "Not unless I'm awfully hungry, and now that I've fucked both of you, 'Princess' sounds a little formal. You boys have my royal permission to just call me 'Manukai' or, better yet, 'Honey Bunch' or 'Baby Doll.' Whose turn is it, by the way? I haven't been laid since San Jose, and it's starting to hurt!"

It was starting to worry Captain Gringo as well. It wasn't that he was a prude. Manukai didn't shock him by wanting to screw all the time. *He* wanted to screw all the time, too. Or at least he did when he wasn't worried about getting killed. It was the big girl's simple approach to sating her simple appetites that had him worried.

They'd had a hell of a time keeping her discreetly inside the coach during the night stops they'd had to make. She hadn't seemed to understand that demanding sex, in English, loudly, even from inside the coach, was not the way one forced Spanish-speaking coachmen and people watering mules late at night to dismiss one as a campesina serving-wench. So was she really fit to mount a top-secret candy store stickup, let alone a risky rescue operation?

He didn't ask her. A guy could only eat the apple a bite at a time, and the first thing they had to do was get her safely out of sight. Luck was with them as Gaston led the way down dark deserted side streets, up an alley, and through the back door of a posada they'd holed up in before.

Naturally, nobody was expecting them. So the landlady greeted them in her nightgown with a candle in one hand and a pepperbox pistol in the other. Then she saw who at least two of them were and heaved a sigh of relief, saying, "Oh, I thought you were burglars, muchachos. You have no idea how pleased I am to see it was only familiar sex fiends picking the lock of my back door. The usual corner suite of rooms?"

Captain Gringo nodded and got out the dough to work things out as Gaston led Manukai upstairs. He told the landlady, "We're sort of on a budget, and the local law's not after us this time, Mamma Rosa. So you just want the going rates for three guests, right?"

"Wrong." Mamma Rosa grinned, displaying a gold front tooth she was sort of proud of and adding, "It is most rude for to shit old friends, Ricardo. You wouldn't have come here if you felt free to enjoy the softer beds and more crowded halls of our finer hotels in Puntarenas. Besides, it is a well-known fact all gringos are muy rico. You pay double as usual, or you take that elephant somewhere else for to fuck, eh?"

He called her a nasty cunt and crossed her palm with silver. She laughed and said, "Bueno. You know the way by now. That is, unless you wish for to come in and have a morning cup of coffee with *me*, Deek."

It was not at all tempting. Mamma Rosa was so ugly, a

good-looking pig would have been more tempting. But he decided he'd better phrase it more delicately, so he winked down at her and said, "I only wish I had the time. But I have to go out again in a few momentos, Querida."

"Oh? It is not you the big India is with? Madre de Dios, there must be more to our little Gaston than one would imagine! I would think he'd need a plank tied across his ass for to keep from falling in, no?"

"Don't be bitchy, Mamma Rosa. It's not her fault her own mamma made her clean the plate every meal when she was still little. I've got to go up and have a few last words with Gaston while he's still got his pants on. It's been nice talking to *you* again."

"Shit." She pouted. "All you *ever* wish for to do with me is talk. Do you not find me at all attractive?"

"I find you muy bonito," he lied, "but you're already charging us more than we can afford, and I really don't have time right now."

"Maybe when you get back?" she suggested wistfully as he turned away to mount the stairs two at a time. When he joined Gaston and Manukai upstairs in the unlit corner suite, the first thing he said was, "I think we've got a problem. Mamma Rosa's got the hots."

Then he saw what Gaston was doing to Manukai on the brass bedstead across the room and added, "Damn it, kiddies, you can go in to play after I go out to contact our people here in Puntarenas! Cut it out, Gaston, I want to talk to Manukai, you pervert!"

The naked giantess spread-eagled on the sagging mattress with Gaston's head between her big brown thighs said, "Don't you dare stop *now*, Frenchie! I can talk and come at the same time, Dick. What's up? I sure hope it's your sweet-loving dong. I'm in the mood for a gang-bang!"

He grimaced and said, "I'm sure you are. Okay, we'll cross our landlady's bridge when someone has to come in it. I want to check out your private navy, Manukai. How do I go about finding it?''

She lay her head back sensuously, eyes closed, and said, ''Oooh, nice! Just go down to the docks and look for a topsail schooner with 'Orotiki' lettered on her bows. The skipper's name is Kuruhai. He speaks English, and he won't eat you if you tell him I sent you. So ... oh ... yessssss!''

Captain Gringo waited politely until she'd finished coming and Gaston had mounted her right to take care of his own needs before he asked the now somewhat calmer princess if there wasn't a more discreet way to contact the schooner, adding, ''A foreign vessel tied up at the main docks like a big-ass bird, with a Kanaka crew aboard, is hardly the best-kept secret in Puntarenas by this late date. Didn't you think to at least run a telephone line ashore?''

''To where, Dick? We noticed people here in Costa Rica sort of noticed us when we sailed in. We're not *that* stupid. I told Kuruhai to keep everyone on board and out of sight as much as possible while I whipped up to the capital to recruit some professional help. I knew we needed some if we ever hope to rescue my people the blackbirders are holding on the Guardian Bank.''

Captain Gringo shook his head wearily and said, ''That's for damned sure. Every move you've made so far was as good as a hand-delivered challenge to the other side. You're as bad as the new young Kaiser of Germany when it comes to telegraphing your punches, Doll. So, okay, your schooner has to be under observation; there's no way any of us can board it without being under observation too, and by now they know what all three of us look like at a distance. Any suggestions, Gaston? Hey Gaston, I'm *talking* to you, Old Buddy!''

Gaston heaved a gasping sigh and managed to mutter,

"It wasn't my fault. She was tearing open my fly before I could shut and bolt the door!"

"Make sure you bolt it after me. Our only hope is to keep them guessing about whether the boss lady is in town yet. They won't expect the schooner and its crew to do anything dramatic until their princess is back on board, and if they haven't mounted a twenty-four hour watch on the gangplank by now they're so stupid we don't have a thing to worry about. I still have to get *myself* aboard. So, any suggestions?"

Gaston was too polite to withdraw from Manukai, but wasn't moving in her as he shook his head and said, "Mais non, I don't see how I could even smuggle my own less interesting public image across the quay and aboard a vessel under constant observation without someone telling Teacher on me, Dick. Not with the sun coming up, at any rate. Perhaps if we just waited here until night falls again?"

Captain Gringo shook his head and said, "I'm sure you could survive another twelve hours of what you're doing right now. But God knows who has what kind of a lead on us already. I'll just have to bull my way through to our own guys and play her by ear. Make sure you don't let anybody catch a single glimpse of the princess here. Don't even let her look out the window. Send out for food, and use the chamber pot under the bed instead of the crapper down the hall, okay?"

"I know how one hides out, Dick. What was that about Mamma Rosa?"

"She made another pass at me just now. I think she's starting to feel left out. Any suggestions?"

"Merde alors, don't look at *me*! Even if I didn't have this adorable child to keep amused, and that is not easy, I'd rather eat *you* than *Mamma Rosa*!"

"Couldn't you just sort of toss her a quick fuck for old

time's sake? She's so hard up, I don't think she'd insist on
the full treatment.''

"Eh bien, *you* toss her the quick fuck then, on your way
out. I am a man who makes love courteously or not at all.
It is not that I am delicate. I'm simply getting too old for
uninspired erections.''

Manukai pouted. "Would you stop bullshitting and
move the one you've got right now some *more,* damn it?''

Captain Gringo snorted in disgust and left. He wasn't
disgusted by what they were doing. He was starting to feel
a little left out, too, as a matter of fact. But, damn it,
somebody around here had to start thinking with his head
instead of his glands if Manukai was at all *serious* about
her mission.

That was something else to worry about as he made his
way to the docks along now painfully illuminated albeit
still deserted streets. How in the hell had even a half-ass
Kanaka king entrusted a mission he had to take halfway
seriously to a daughter as dumb as Manukai, unless, of
course, she was as smart as they *came,* at his court?

There were times for a soldier of fortune to seek his
fortune, and there were times when he had to think first of
his own ass. This was starting to look like the latter. But,
what the hell, they'd come this far, so he might as well at
least see how hopeless it really was.

The docks were beginning to come to life as he reached
the waterfront. It wasn't hard to find the Orotiki. For,
though schooner-rigged, she was the biggest sailing vessel
in the harbor. She was a Clyde-built steel-hulled two-
hundred-footer with auxiliary power as well as sails. The
long black hull looked sinister enough without the figure-
head resembling a wooden Indian carved by someone
having a nightmare. An unguarded gangplank led down to
the wharf. So he went up it.

A female Kanaka deckhand, if that's what she was,

wearing what looked like a big kerchief around her hips, a flower in her hair, and nothing else, smiled at him and called out in her own melodious lingo. A big, heavyset island guy appeared in the open hatchway of the quarter-deck and called out, "Aloha, Haole Blalah, what the fuck you want?"

Captain Gringo called back the princess had sent him as he approached the big Kanaka. The skipper, for that's what his hat said he was, was young and good-looking, if one liked lantern jaws and heavy brows that met in the middle. He was wearing a white linen panama suit, with no shirt under the jacket and no shoes on his big brown feet. He admitted he was Captain Kuruhai as they shook on it. Then he suggested they talk in his cabin. Captain Gringo said, "Hold the thought. We were spotted by the other side up in San Jose, and if we didn't lose them, another vessel could be putting out for the Guardian Bank any time now."

Kuruhai shouted an order in Kanaka, and a vahine Captain Gringo hadn't noticed up to now started up the shrouds to the lookout's crow's nest hand over hand. It was hard to see how he'd failed to notice her. She was naked as a jay, built like a brick shithouse, and moving her hula hips pretty good as she climbed. It was a swell way to avoid attracting attention in a conservative Catholic seaport. But at least she'd spot the dispatch vessel if they'd already attracted attention from the wrong people.

Both tall men had to duck as they went inside, although Kuruhai wasn't quite so tall as Princess Manukai. The skipper's cabin was Spartan but roomy, with a chart table set up in the center and built-in cupboards and bunks all around. Kuruhai mixed rum and coconut water for them both as Captain Gringo brought him up to date. The big Kanaka handed the American his drink, sat down with his own, and said, "Ain' no big thing, Blalah. Suppose you got Princess Manukai down safe to the coast, we just gotta get her on board, cast off, and go get them fucking blackbirders chop-chop.''

Captain Gringo said, "It's not quite that simple. I sort of like to plan my battles in advance. For openers, do you have a map of the area we're talking about?''

Kuruhai nodded, turned on his stool near the chart table, and reached a long arm out to snag a rolled-up nautical chart from a nearby shelf. He spread it on the table between them, saying, "Royal Navy. The Lime Juicers draw the best ones. Don't never sail the South Pacific with no *Frog* chart. The Frogs are better artists than mapmakers.''

Captain Gringo stared down at the British version of the Guardian Bank. It looked sort of as if someone had outlined a banana with a dotted line. If the scale was right, the oval of reefs and islets was about sixty miles long by twenty across. If those dots were dry land, there wasn't one hell of a lot of it. Kuruhai put a big brown finger on the chart, covering at least half a dozen dots, and said, "Our boy who got away thinks the people we have to rescue are being held on a maybe five hundred acre rock about here.''

Captain Gringo frowned and asked, "He can't pin down the exact island out of at least a hundred? I'd better have a chat with him.''

Kuruhai said, "You can't. He's back on Konakona, getting over the fevers he picked up in these waters. He wouldn't be any good to you if he was here, Blalah. Them rocks out there don't have no names, and they all look alike. The boy said him and the others had been diving off a bitty pancake of coral rock, with more of the same north and south, when he got sick of working for Haoles for nothing and went into the swimming business for himself.''

"Oboy. At least he was sure the slavers were Germans, though?''

Kuruhai shook his massive head and said, "No, *we* are. The kids them blackbirders lured aboard a schooner with toys and candy wouldn't know a German from a Greek. All you pink Haoles look alike to uneducated Kanakas. But us aristocrats who read can put two and two together no matter what the missionaries say about the way we screw. So it was no big thing to figure out a German-owned pearling syndicate had to be run by Germans, see? Wait, I got their business card here someplace."

He half rose, rummaged in a drawer, and produced a card reading, "Halle und Feldmacher, Bremerhaven," with finer additional print neither could even try to make sense out of. Kuruhai said, "We asked other Haole traders we deal with about them. They're known as crooks by all the other South Pacific trading companies, and you should see how the ones who *don't* grab our people try to cheat us in business! That's why King Kamamamoku sent his daughter to the mainland to get educated Haole-style. It's a big pain in the ass to trade with people who consider you an easy lay."

Captain Gringo suppressed a laugh. For though it could hardly be said Princess Manukai had learned to preserve her virtue, he grasped the sense of what the Kanaka meant. He said, "Okay, if Halle and Feldmacher are known crooks working the pearl banks of the Guardian Bank with forced labor, they have to be blackbirders or at least working with blackbirders."

Kuruhai nodded and said, "Let's not worry about the fine print. Let's go *kill* the cocksuckers!"

"Hold the thought. Like I said, it's a good idea to start with at least a half-assed plan and, as of the moment, we're not even sure which way to go, while they seem to be expecting us to drop by. So while we're trying to decide which island to invade, they've had days to set up their *defenses*!"

"You pink people sure do worry a lot. When our old kings wanted to invade an island, they just loaded up their catamarans, said the proper prayers to the tikis, and hit the beach singing their war songs!"

Captain Gringo shrugged and said, "That's probably why us pink people own all your bigger islands these days. We worry as much as you say we do. We call it military science."

"Bullshit, *we* call it guns and numbers. The clap your whalers and missionaries brought us along with trade liquor and Jesus shaved the odds for you guys a lot, too, you know."

Captain Gringo took another sip of the hardly weak refreshments his host had provided before he said, "Let's not argue about that. I don't own one square inch of anyone's land, and we're really agreeing about the art of war. How many guns do we have to work with, for openers?"

Kuruhai said, "We've a hundred repeating rifles in the hold, with nearly ten thousand rounds of ammo, a couple of cases of dynamite, and of course a cutlass for everyone on board."

Captain Gringo nodded thoughtfully and said, "That's not bad. Princess Manukai said you had fifty fighting men. If they hadn't stolen her checkbook, it might have been possible to recruit some out-of-work Costa Rican soldados too."

Kuruhai chuckled and said, "Oh, that Manukai. There she goes again with her mainland suffragette ideas. We don't have fifty *men*. We have two dozen men and their *vahines*. But the princess seems to think women are just as tough as men. Some of them may be. But not *all* Kanaka girls grow as big as the royal family!"

"Ouch!" said Captain Gringo, adding: "Okay, that means we need at least seventy-five extra men if we want men holding all hundred of those rifles. I have an open mind about Miss Virginia Woodhull and her notions of females holding male jobs. But I'm not about to lead untrained hula dancers into battle against professional thugs of undetermined strength!''

He took another sip of his drink and said, "Shit, if only we had some *money* to work with. I suppose the princess could draw more from the bank here in Puntarenas on her signature, but if I was a slaver who knew she was after me and I'd already stolen her purse, I'd be *expecting* her to make for one of the few international banks in town, and they already tried to kill her once!''

The skipper said, "Hey, that's no big thing, Blalah. How much money do you need?''

"You got money?''

"Sure we got money. What you suppose we pay people as we sail around these waters, seashells?''

The skipper put his glass down, got up, and moved to haul a sea chest out from under a bunk. He opened it. Captain Gringo whistled. The good-size chest was filled almost to the brim with gold and silver coins. The Kanaka said, "We got British Sovs, Mex Birds, Yankee Cartwheels, even Maria Theresa Dollars they don't make no more. King Kamamamoku don't take none of that *paper* shit for his pearls and copra, see?''

"I see indeed! You've got enough specie there to fund a modest war! So, okay, we don't have to risk Manukai's fair hide in the open after all. I may as well pick up *two* machine guns along with a guerrilla army of, say, seventy-five. My pal, Gaston, will know the trustworthy arms merchants and knockaround guys here in Puntarenas. So give me at least a thousand in gold, and I'll get started right away.''

Kuruhai closed the sea chest, shoved it back under the bunk, and straightened up to ask, pleasantly enough, "Do

I really look like a vahine you can fuck for a fishhook,
Haole? You don't get shit till Princess Manukai tells me
she really *knows* you! My daddy gave a thousand acres of
good taro land one time to a missionary who said it was
for Jesus. Only, we ain't seen Jesus on the property yet.
We've wised up a bit since then."

Captain Gringo chuckled and said, "I see why you're
still living under native rule. Okay, we'd better go ashore
and have a word with her highness, then. Like I said, we
have her safely under cover at a posada up the slope."

The big Kanaka opened another drawer, took out a
snub-nose S&W .32, and put it into the side pocket of his
jacket as he said, "Let's go then."

They did. The naked lady lookout shouted down, when
asked, that she hadn't seen anything bigger than a rowboat
putting out to sea against the tide, so far.

The skipper yelled at everyone else to man the main
brace, swab the deck, or whatever he meant in Kanaka.
Then he and Captain Gringo went ashore and headed south
along the quay. Kuruhai asked how far they had to go, and
Captain Gringo explained, "Farther than we really have
to. In case someone's gazing at our backs right now, I
want them to think we have your princess down *this* way,
see?"

"You don't?"

"No. The posada I told you about is actually northeast
of your schooner. But it's still cool; the side streets will be
even cooler; and I've been here before, so I know a few
alleyways *I'd* sure as hell have a time tailing anyone
through without him spotting me."

They came to a waterfront chandler's shop he and
Gaston knew. He led the Kanaka inside, nodded pleasantly
to the chandler waiting on a customer, and just kept going
out the back door. As they moved up a narrow, shaded
alley, Kuruhai chuckled and said, "I'm beginning to see

why the princess hired you, Blalah. Are you always this sneaky?"

"Only when I'm worried about being followed, which is most of the time. Hold it."

The Kanaka stood bemused as Captain Gringo looked both ways before opening a massive oaken gate, saying, "We can cut through this old churchyard to the next street. Nobody ever seems to be around on weekdays. Found this shortcut the hard way, when I had to, last time I was chased through Puntarenas."

Kuruhai waited until they were cutting back the other way along the side street beyond the church grounds before he asked, "Do you really know this town? I mean, do you know the *vahines* here?"

"Not all of them, and by the way, they prefer to be called señoritas. What's the problem? You've only got two dozen naked Kanaka girls aboard your schooner."

Kuruhai sighed and said, "There's twenty-six, and it sure does give a man a hard-on."

Captain Gringo laughed incredulously and asked, "Are you trying to tell me the skipper of a half-female crew can't get laid, Kuruhai?"

The young skipper growled, "I ain't *trying* to tell you, damn it. I'm telling you! I had a couple of native girls at our last port of call. But the vahines aboard Orotiki are tapu to me, and it's starting to hurt like hell!"

"I can see how it would, considering how modestly they dress! But if every woman on board is off limits, why the hell did you bring them along?"

"That's really stupid, even coming from a Haole! Didn't anyone ever tell you us Kanakas are a passionate race?"

"I have heard rumors to that effect. But you just said all those girls were tapu, so . . ."

"Tapu to *me,* not to the other guys in the crew. I'm from the royal clan. Common people aren't even allowed to eat with me. I'm only allowed to screw royalty or, of course, people who don't follow the same gods. So about the vahines here in Puntarenas . . ."

Captain Gringo started to say he wasn't a pimp, for God's sake. Then he grinned and said, "As a matter of fact, Gaston and I have been trying to figure out how to get our landlady fixed up, before she calls the law on us. It's only fair to warn you, though. She's ugly as a mud fence."

Kuruhai brightened and asked, "Are you sure she really wants to get laid? Who cares what she looks like, as long as I can have some nukinuki without breaking tapu! I'm so hard up I'd screw a pig right now!"

Captain Gringo chuckled and said, "Well, Mamma Rosa walks on her hind legs, at least." He didn't think it polite to add he didn't think that was a hell of an improvement. Kuruhai could always say no, once he had a look at the poor old hag.

They zigzagged on, stopping now and again to make sure they weren't followed. Then they ducked in the back way to discover, as they met Mamma Rosa in the lobby of her posada, that they'd been wasting their time trying to make sure nobody knew where the princess was staying.

Mamma Rosa pointed to the expensive set of matching luggage just inside the front door and said, "An hombre dropped these things off for the lady upstairs just a few momentos ago. I tried for to tell her. But every time I rap on the door, that Gaston tells me for to go away, most rudely!"

Captain Gringo stared soberly down at the luggage and asked Kuruhai if he recognized the bags. The Kanaka nodded and said, "Sure, it's no big thing. She took them with her up to San Jose. But didn't you say somebody *stole* her things when they blew up her room?"

Captain Gringo sighed and said, "I don't know what the

hell they're trying to tell us now. Wait here. I'll take these bags up and see what Manukai has to say about them.''

"I'll help," offered Kuruhai. But Captain Gringo told him to stay with Mamma Rosa for now as he picked up the bags and started up the stairs with them. This tapu shit was a little complicated, and he wasn't sure whether the princess wanted to be seen in the feathers with Gaston by a subject—or whatever Kuruhai was to her. As he left them together, he heard Kuruhai telling Mamma Rosa what a great pair of tits she had. So, apparently, he really *was* hard up enough to lay a pig.

Captain Gringo got to the locked door and kicked it, calling out, "Open up, goddamn it. We got troubles!"

That got Gaston out of bed and the princess pretty good. As the naked little Frenchman opened the door, he sighed and said, "Thank heavens you've returned, Dick. This child is insatiable!"

Captain Gringo told him to bolt the fucking door as he carried the bags over to the bed. Manukai was only taking up half the mattress with her brown naked charms. So he placed the bags on the bed and asked her if they were the ones she'd lost in San Jose.

She said, "They sure look like the same ones," as she popped the latch to open the nearest one. Captain Gringo shouted, *"No!"* But it was too late.

Fortunately, no bomb went off as the princess raised the top to say, "Oh look, here's my handbag too, in with my clothes!"

"Don't open that!" he warned. But she already had, to dump the contents between her naked knees as she knelt on the bed. She said, "Oh shit, my checkbook and passport are still missing!"

Gaston had come over to rejoin them. He said, "Eh bien, obviously they were less interested in your personal clothing, since, after all, how many thieves have girl

friends they might *fit*? But I still find it très unusual for a
thief to go to so much trouble, hein? Why carry purloined
luggage all the way from San Jose just to give it back?''

Captain Gringo growled, ''Easy. They just had to pick it
up and carry it. They returned it as a *message*.''

Manukai frowned up at him and asked, ''What kind of a
message, Dick? I don't get it!''

He said, ''I'm not sure I do, either. But they obviously
wanted us to know they knew where we were!''

Gaston frowned and said, ''It only works one way, my
children. We are dealing with *two* sets of spooks!''

Manukai was more surprised to hear this than Captain
Gringo. The tall American nodded and said, ''Right.
People who throw bombs don't try to scare anyone off.
Whoever sent those thugs to warn us off must have sent
these things back as a further warning. The guys who tried
to kill you with high explosives weren't fucking around.''

Manukai smiled sensuously and said, ''Speaking of
fucking around, whose turn is it with me?''

Both soldiers of fortune looked equally dismayed at her
suggestion. Gaston said, ''Sacre bleu, you wayward child,
aside from the fact I just made you come again less than
five minutes ago, even you must have grasped by now that
your adorable big brown derriere is in dire danger!''

She said, ''Oh pooh, Dick just said that whoever dropped
my things off just now was simply being silly. Damn it,
I'm still *hot*!''

Captain Gringo moved over to a basket of fruit on the
dresser, handed her a banana, and said, ''Here. Us boys
have to do some serious thinking and . . . Oh, by the way,
your subject Kuruhai is right downstairs and hard up as hell,
if he's not tapu to you.''

Manukai sighed and said, ''As a matter of fact, he is. I
outrank him, even if we are of the same royal clan. What's
he doing here?''

"Laying Mamma Rosa by now, most likely. I brought him along to get your permission to spend some of your treasure chest on arms and recruits. But hold that thought. We've got other worries right now!"

He moved to the window facing the street as Gaston did the same with the one facing the passageway through the block on that side of their corner room. As Captain Gringo peered through the slats to see nothing but a couple of kids whipping a top in the calle below, he mused aloud, "If they meant to attack in broad-ass daylight, they'd have done so already. Up until a minute ago they'd have been able to literally catch you alone with your pants down. Now there are three armed men on the premises for them to worry about."

Gaston sighed and said, "That is only just. I am most worried about *them*, too. I am très confuse as well. How could they have gotten those bags from Manukai's room after the explosion if they were not guests at the same hotel, Dick?"

"They probably were. But they didn't grab that expensive leather *after* a bomb went off in the same small room with them!"

"Ah, oui, there is not a scratch on the leather. So someone stole her things just after we left to find a more substantial bed. Then the other ones avec the boom-boom arrived within minutes to behave in an even less civilized manner, hein?"

"Yeah. But which is which? I can see someone working for the blackbirders either trying to scare us off or kill us. But I'll be switched if I can figure out who *else* is involved, or why."

"Try it this way, Dick. What if only one group simply does not give the shit how they stop us, either by frightening or killing us and—Mais non, that simply makes no sense."

Captain Gringo nodded and said, "Not unless we're

dealing with a nuthead. You don't warn people before you try to blow them up. You don't leave luggage for an impulsive lady to open *without* a bomb inside, unless you just don't have a bomb handy. I'd better run down and get Kuruhai. No matter what the hell's going on, we've got to either fort up or get *out* of here!''

He turned to see that Manukai had taken his sarcastic suggestion seriously. He sighed and said, "Princess, take that fucking banana out of your snatch and put some clothes on. I'll be right back with company, damn it.''

He didn't wait to see if she was paying him any attention. He knew Gaston would get them both dressed, once the big dumb broad came; and from the way she was moving that fruit, it didn't figure to take her long.

He went back downstairs. The small lobby was empty and Mamma Rosa's door was closed. He knocked on it, got no answer, and tried the latch. Mamma Rosa hadn't locked the door.

He could see, as he opened it, she'd been in too great a hurry. It sure looked silly to see a skinny, wrinkled mestiza bouncing up and down atop a big brown walrus. Kuruhai grinned up at him and said, "I owe you, Blalah. This little Haole vahine moves her pussy like it's pounding poi! You want seconds?''

Captain Gringo said, "No thanks. When you kids finish coming, come on upstairs and be sure you bring your gun. We may have to fight our way out of here.''

Mamma Rosa groaned. "Can't we talk about fighting later, damn it? I haven't enjoyed such good fucking in years!''

But her supine lover said, "Just keep moving, you sweet little thing. The man says we may have some fighting to do. But that's no big thing. Us Kanakas can screw, eat, and fight all at the same time. When you want to start fighting our way out of here, Haole Blalah?''

Captain Gringo took out his pocket watch and said, "Before the streets are deserted for La Siesta. That's if somebody doesn't try to fight their way in *before* then, of course. So, no shit, we'd better get moving."

The big Kanaka chuckled, rolled Mamma Rosa over on her back, and said, "You heard the man, vahine. What say I show you how to *move*, Kanaka style?"

Everyone makes more sense when sexually satisfied and wearing clothes. So even the princess had calmed down at least a little as Captain Gringo called the strategy session to order.

Having only three armed men and two sort of dotty women to man the defenses was the first order of business. Mamma Rosa said there were iron grilles over all the few windows downstairs, and that before coming up she and Kuruhai had barred both the front and back entrances. But she added that her other working-class posada guests were going to be mad as hell when they came home for La Siesta to find themselves locked out in the noonday sun.

Captain Gringo nodded and said, "Bueno. That's when we'll make our move. Anyone aiming to hit us hard enough to worry about will want to move in either well before La Siesta, while the streets are half empty, or well after La Siesta starts, when they're *completely* deserted. They won't want to make their move while everyone's pushing and shoving their way home to hit the sack. So that's when we stand the best chance of busting out without getting shot."

He turned to Gaston to ask, "What's the best hotel in town, the Casa Real?" and Gaston said, "I don't know if it's the best, but it's the most expensive. Mais pourquoi?

Are we not planning a très dramatique dash for the ship, Dick?''

"Kuruhai and I have to head for the schooner whether it's under observation or not. But I want you to run the princess to the hotel and hole her up there.''

"Mon dieu! How many times in one day do you expect a man my age to hole anybody? Why can't *you* check into a new love nest avec this sweet little thing?''

Manukai grinned and said, "Ooh, that sounds like fun!''

Captain Gringo shook his head and said, "Anyone watching the gangplank has already seen me going aboard and vice-versa. It couldn't be helped. But they haven't seen you and Gaston boarding the vessel yet, and until they do, they won't be expecting us to do anything important. They know the owner of the Orotiki is in town. But if she's checked into the finest hotel in town, with a week's rent paid in advance, they won't know what the hell to think and, meanwhile, might not *do* anything while they try to figure it out, see?''

Manukai nodded, but objected, "If I don't have my checkbook and you don't want me going to the bank, how am I to pay a day in advance, let alone a week, Dick?''

Kuruhai reached into his pocket, took out a big brown fistful of gold coins, and said, "Ain't no big thing, Princess,'' as he handed her the small fortune.

Captain Gringo nodded and said, "Once you're safely locked in at the hotel, don't even let Room Service in unless one of us is there with a gun as well as you. We'd better contact the main office of International Express and warn them about your stolen checkbook. That can wait until after La Siesta. Nobody could hang much paper with all the banks and shops in town closed. Maybe we can pick up a new passport for you at . . . Oboy, what kind of a passport does a citizen of a South Sea Island travel under, anyway?''

She said, ''French, of course. Konakona doesn't issue passports. When strangers sail in, we either invite them for supper or *have* them for supper, depending on how friendly they look to us. But since you pink people are so fussy, I picked up a courtesy visa from the French on Tahiti as I was leaving for the mainland. It was only a little out of my way, anyway.''

Kuruhai frowned thoughtfully and asked, ''What does she need a new passport for *now*, Blalah? Once she's back aboard Orotiki, she's in Konakona territory; and once we rescue our people, she'll be heading home with the rest of us. It's going to be sort of crowded in the hold if we manage to save *half* them kidnapped pearl divers. So we sure won't want to put in at any *other* port, see?''

Captain Gringo nodded but said, ''Just the same, we'd better notify the French government someone else is wandering around with Manukai's stolen ID. You want to cover that bet, Gaston? Your French is a lot better than mine.''

Gaston smiled crookedly and replied, ''Surely you jest. My French is good indeed, but for some reason the French government seems to think I have been a bad boy. Let them *keep* the stolen passport. What good will it do anyone but a female standing six-foot-six who, when asked, speaks fluent Polynesian, dirty?''

Captain Gringo chuckled at the mental picture of a less unusual lady gang member trying to explain her passport to anyone important and said, ''Okay, I'll wire my old pal Olivia about the checkbook, at least, when I get the chance. Meanwhile, since you're semi-invisible in a crowd as well as shy, Gaston, I want you to secure the princess at the hotel, then slip out during La Siesta and see if you can contact any rogues you know here in Puntarenas.''

Gaston shrugged and said, "I know beaucoup vaguely sinister people here, and La Siesta is the discreet time of the day to tap on doors. Mais what am I to ask for, the time of day?"

"We need a couple of machine guns. Maxims if you can get 'em. Brownings if you can't. But don't let anyone sell you a Hotchkiss or Spandau, for God's sake. They'll probably be chambered for thirty-thirty. What kind of ammo do we have aboard the Orotiki, Kuruhai?"

The big Kanaka said, "You name it, we got it. Plenty of thirty-thirty for the Krags we brought. Forty-four-forty for the Winchesters. Shotguns are all ten and twelve gauge."

It wouldn't have been polite, or done any good at this late date, to tell Kuruhai what he thought of arming troops with mixed weapons. So he just nodded and told Gaston, "We'll need at least a couple of dozen belts for each machine gun. Try to get more."

"Avec what? My personal signature, Dick? I know two arms dealers here in Puntarenas, but I don't know one who extends credit to his mother!"

"Tell 'em it's cash on delivery. I don't pay people I don't know in advance, either. After you arrange the weapons deal, contact a guerrilla employment agency and see if you can line up at least three platoons of old pros. Make sure the squad leaders at least are guys you know."

"Eh bien, but what about the guns and ammo for such a très formidable gang, Dick?"

"If they don't have their own guns and ammo, what the fuck *good* are they to anybody? Don't tell anyone just what the deal is. But let them know it's a no-shit all-out attack that should be over, one way or the other, in less than twenty-four. Don't try to con anybody. We don't want to recruit any sissies."

He turned to Manukai and asked, "Can we offer a hundred a day to the leaders, with the bucks drawing fifty?

We're talking real dough, I know, but we want trained fighting men, not guys who shoot all the pigs and chickens, yell 'viva' a lot, and run away.''

She nodded, and Kuruhai said, "Ain't no big thing. We got over a million U.S. in my cabin alone. Wait till you see what the princess here has in *her* sea chest.''

Captain Gringo said, "I wish *I* owned some coconuts and a pearl bed. But we're still not out of the woods, even if and when we get out of here.''

He took out his watch, consulted it, and told Mamma Rosa, "You'd better go down and let anyone you know in. It's about time for the goldbricks to start knocking off early.''

She nodded, but asked, "Can Kuruhai come with me, Deek? I am so helpless, a mere woman alone.''

Captain Gringo said, "He's already come with you enough for now. And you're about as helpless as a basket of cobras, Mamma Rosa. Even if you weren't, nobody's after *you*. Once we're gone, you'll be back in business as usual. So go downstairs and tend to your business, damn it!''

She left, muttering that her business could use at least another good screwing. Captain Gringo moved to the window and, yeah, a couple of dock workers were moving along the narrow walk down there now. He said, "We'll give it another few minutes. Then Kuruhai and I pop out the back while you pop out the front with the princess and make a run for the hotel, Gaston. Leave her luggage here for now. We can have it delivered to her later.''

Kuruhai frowned and asked, "Wouldn't it be better if the princess snuck out the back way, Blalah?'' So Captain Gringo told him, "They know she's in here and that there are only two ways she can leave. She'll be a lot safer out on a crowded street than in an alley, see?''

"Yeah, I see it *now*. But how safe are *you* and *me* gonna be in that back alley, Blalah?"

"I don't know. That's why we're the ones who have to chance it."

Nothing happened when Captain Gringo and Kuruhai left the posada via the back alley. Since they heard no shots echoing from anywhere else, they could only assume Gaston and the big girl had made it, too. They still felt a lot safer once they'd circled to a main calle leading to the waterfront and forged west against the crowd of homecomers. Kuruhai kept looking back to see if he could see if they were being followed. Captain Gringo knew better than to try, in this crowd.

They knew their earlier pussyfoot to the posada had been wasted effort. So they beelined for the schooner and were soon back aboard. The casual deck watch, this time a male Kanaka, also wearing a flower in his hair, said nobody had bothered them or even tried to come aboard. So Kuruhai said there was a lot to be said for this siesta shit and headed for his cabin to inhale some booze and recover from the effects of all the excitement and Mamma Rosa.

Captain Gringo had shared the excitement, but was starting to feel a little left out, now that he'd seen what Mamma Rosa looked like with her shabby clothes off. Gaston had once observed that women with ugly faces proved Darwin's theory. The human race was descended from people who'd been running around bare-ass until recently. So for thousands of years, the guys had been judging female beauty more on the basis of tits and ass than faces; and so, until recently, ugly girls with great bodies had been having most of the kids.

The guy seated on a nail keg by the gangplank wasn't at all attractive, even half naked, and worse yet, he spoke neither Spanish nor English. So the still-keyed-up American moved to the shrouds and started climbing for a bird's-eye view of his surroundings. It was one hell of a climb, even for a man who wasn't afraid of heights. He was sweating by the time he climbed into the crow's nest and found it occupied by a naked vahine instead of a crow. He smiled at her and said, "Howdy. Have you spotted anything moving in or out of the harbor so far?"

The Kanaka girl smiled at him, mystified, and replied in her own lingo, which was a lot of help. He said, "Never mind. I'll figure it out for myself," as he gazed all around at the view from up here.

Nothing much seemed to be going on, either out on the glassy waters or among the red-tiled buildings ashore. The tropic sun was directly above, and the canvas-walled platform would have been a bake oven at this time of day had not a pleasant sea breeze been blowing at this altitude. The naked brown vahine was still in better shape to catch the breeze with her curves than he was in his sweaty jacket, however. So he took it off and hung it over the circular pipe rail of the cockpit. The breeze felt marvelous on his damp shirt. But it felt even better when he hung his gun rig and both the shirt and his straw hat on an overhead fitting to dry. His actions had been innocent in intent. But he suspected, when the naked vahine wrapped her soft brown arms around him and leaned her head back for a kiss, that she might have misunderstood his actions just now.

Or had she? A guy would have had to be pretty dumb to misunderstand *her* intentions as she rubbed her little brown hips and black V of love fuzz against his pants, still obviously waiting to be kissed. So he kissed her and, yeah, it was true that flat noses didn't seem to matter so much when the rest a lady had to offer was so pretty.

Save for skin coloring and sexual enthusiasm, this Kanaka girl was not at *all* like the big princess. She stood less than five-foot-four in her dainty bare feet and weighed maybe a hundred and ten, all of it firm and athletic. Even her naked cupcakes felt solid as muscle against his naked flesh as she teased her nipples in his chest hair. She kissed great too, so he could hardly wait to find out what else she could do when she, obviously as curious, proceeded to reach down with one hand to unbutton his pants. He started to work his belt loose too, saying, "Let me help. What's your name, Sweet Stuff?"

She didn't seem to understand the question. Once they had his pants down, it didn't seem important to him either. The bottom of the crow's nest was a hardwood grid that would have been as rough on her brown butt as a waffle iron. So he swung her around with her back to the mast to try for a wall job—or, in this case, mast job?

Whatever it was, she seemed to enjoy it as he bent his knees to enter her frontally, standing up. She gasped in surprised pleasure as she felt what he had to offer in her warm, wet depths. But to help him get it all the way in, she had to be a bit ingenious, so she was. He laughed as she raised her legs one at a time to hook the arches of her bare feet on the rail behind him to either side and slide herself higher up the mast.

As he straightened his legs to start humping her more comfortably as well as deeper, he asked, "Have you done this often up here? Never mind, I don't really want to know. This is neat. We can watch the whole port as we screw up here, and with that canvas as high as my hips, nobody can watch us. Or at least they can't be *sure* what they're watching, right?"

She leaned her head back against the mast, eyes closed, and seemed to be telling him she loved him, or maybe she was threatening his life while she moved her wide-open crotch astoundingly in apparent defiance of gravity.

Whatever she was saying sure sounded passionate enough to account for what the rest of her was doing. He ejaculated in her and kept going—it was easy as well as common courtesy with such a skilled partner in such an interesting position. But when she came in turn, hissing like a steam valve and biting her lower lip, she fell off his shaft and slid weakly down the mast to lie in a ball at his feet, moaning that he'd killed her . . . or at least that she'd had enough for now. He supposed people who tore off casual sex with strangers a lot, with neither shame nor a need for a big buildup, probably took the whole deal as fleeting pleasure, the way his kind took a snack.

He said, "Okay, you don't want to make a full-course meal out of it, I won't pester you for dessert. A guy's got to keep his strength up, anyway."

She looked up at him, her big brown eyes confused. He reached down to pat her cheek, saying, "Don't try to figure it out, Honey. Maybe this is the best way, when you study on it. Most of the things men and women feel required to say to one another when they're fucking are a little stupid anyway. Our brains are built as different as our bodies, and . . ." Then he spotted something coming in over the harbor bar and swore, "Oh, son of a baby-raping bitch!"

The girl at his feet whimpered and cowered away, frightened as well as confused by his obvious if mysterious annoyance. He shook his head down at her and said, "It's not you. It's what's coming our way under a full head of steam! Get up. I'll show you."

She wasn't about to rise high enough to get slugged by a big Haole maniac who growled so at vahines. But to appease him she reached shly up to fondle his balls. He laughed and said, "*Now* you tell me you want more. Come on, I won't hurt you."

He pulled her to her feet and pointed. It was her turn to gasp and probably cuss in Kanaka as she saw the long gray gunboat moving into the harbor. On shore, someone was firing a ceremonial salute, and one of the gunboat's smaller deck guns was puffing white smoke as it fired its own blanks politely. A white, or mostly white, ensign fluttered from the yardarm above the conning tower as well. It was the battle flag of the German Kriegsmarine! He said, "That tears it. They've taken off the gloves."

His softer and sweeter fellow lookout turned to him with a puzzled stare. He said, "Never mind," and patted his own chest, saying, "Me Dick, savvy?"

She brightened, put a hand to one perky breast, and said, "Me Likelike."

He laughed and said, "That's for sure, whether we're talking about your name or your manners. I have to go below, Likelike. It's been nice, ah, talking to you."

He started to get dressed again. She pouted, held her breasts out to him, and managed, "No! Likelike wanna make nukinuki with mo' Dick!"

He sighed and said, "You dames just never want to do it when a man has the time, I wanna nukinuki you some more, too. But Jesus, Likelike, we're really in real trouble now!"

Kuruhai agreed, when Captain Gringo roused him out on deck. But after a while it seemed obvious that whatever the German gunboat intended, it didn't seem to be aiming its big guns at Orotiki. They waited until it had dropped anchor out in the roads and had sent a launch ashore farther down the waterfront before Captain Gringo told the big Kanaka, "Sit tight. I'd better go ashore and see what I can find out. I can't see even Der Kaiser acting really raw in a banana port under Uncle Sam's protection."

"What if you're wrong?" asked Kuruhai. So Captain Gringo shrugged and said, "Give up without resistance, and maybe the princess can bail you out. You're not about to stand off an armored steamer armed with one-fifty-fives! But, as you say, it's probably no big thing as long as we're in the harbor."

"You mean they'll come after us as we *leave*?"

"Wouldn't *you* do it that way if you were a German skipper trying to protect a German-owned pearling outfit? Let's not waste time *talking* about it. Let's try to find out what the fuck's really going on!"

He moved down the gangplank before anyone off the gunboat could move that far up the quay. He moved directly across to the first cross street and made tracks for the Hotel Casa Real. La Siesta was, of course, well under way. So the streets were deserted, or he thought they were until he heard running footsteps behind him. He ducked into a doorway and turned to look back from modest cover. Two burly guys dressed blanco were moving his way pretty good, making no attempt to conceal their intent or the clubs in their hands. Captain Gringo swore softly and reached for the .38 under his jacket. He didn't make it. As the door behind him popped suddenly inward and somebody slugged him from behind, hard, he only had time to groan, "Oh shit, *suckered*!" before everything around him went dark for a while.

• • •

When he came to, not knowing where or when, Captain Gringo found himself stretched out on a leather couch in what looked like an oak-paneled office. He was unbound, but when he felt for his .38, unarmed as well. His hat lay on a coffee table between him and a tall figure leaning against the only door he could see from the couch—even when he sat up, felt the back of his throbbing head, and muttered, "I'll get you for this, Von Linderhoff."

The sardonic, scar-faced, one-eyed Prussian intelligence agent he'd tangled with in the past chuckled fondly and said, "So good of you to drop by, Walker. I thought it was about time we had a little talk, nicht wahr?"

"I'll nick your wahr the next time I catch you with your back to *me*, you tricky bastard! You set me up pretty good with that one doorway in sight when your bit players entered stage left."

Von Linderhoff shrugged modestly and replied, "*I* thought so. You are not an easy man to take alive, you know."

"Okay, so consider me took. What happens now, you Prussian prick?"

"Ach, Herr Walker, is that any way to talk to an old friend? As you may recall, you spared *my* life one time when the shoe was on the other foot. I only wanted to return the favor."

"You mean you clobbered me to keep your navy from sinking me?"

The German laughed and said, "You are not far off the mark. We have, as you may have suspected, been watching the odd behavior of the Princess Manukai for some time with considerable interest. Until you and Gaston Verrier joined forces with those crazy Kanakas, we had little to worry about. Unfortunately, you two soldiers of fortune could confuse an already complicated game further. So let us discuss business, Herr Walker. Just how much do you want to, ah, get up from the table?"

Captain Gringo shook his head to clear it, reached in his jacket, and found nobody had swiped his smokes. He took out a claro and fumbled for a light as he muttered, "Let me get this straight, Von Linderhoff. You're offering us a *bribe*? You're not turning me over to the American consulate here in Puntarenas for the money they'd be willing to pay *you*?"

Von Linderhoff moved forward to light his cigar courteously as he said, "I am already on a generous expense account, and we both know a hangman's noose awaits you back in the United States. Can't you see I am trying to be your friend, ah, Dick?"

"Just call me Herr Walker. 'Friend' is putting things a little cute, Squarehead."

"Nonetheless, we have made deals in the past when it was in both our interests, and on one occasion I shall never forget, you spared my life when you could have killed me. Whatever we may think of one another, we are both officers and gentlemen, nicht wahr?"

Captain Gringo got his claro going good before he said grudgingly, "Okay, I've never caught you in an outright fib, and I've always kept my word with you. I gave my word to Princess Manukai, too. Even if I hadn't, I can't see selling out a mess of innocent natives to your higher *kulture*, you blackbirding Bavarian bastard!"

"*Prussian*, if you please!" Von Linderhoff sighed, adding: "Whether you admire the Second Reich or not, I assure you Der Kaiser does not approve of mistreating natives, even in his African colonies."

"That's not the way the *Africans* tell it. But let's get back to the South Pacific. You spike-helmeted assholes don't even own the island those pearl divers were kidnapped from!"

"It is our understanding they are contract laborers work-

ing for private German interests, not the German *government*,
Herr Walker.''

"So let's see their contracts, and how come your
government's interested at all if it has nothing to do with
slave-raiding?''

Von Linderhoff sat on the couch beside him, giving him
a free shot at the distant door; but he decided to listen
awhile anyway. The wiry Kraut could move fast as hell, he
knew, and he knew he was still groggy. So even though he
knew it was a lot of bullshit, he held still for Von
Linderhoff's saying, "Seriously, Walker, Der Kaiser *does*
have interests in the South Pacific. More important interests than the fate of a few unwashed savages. We have, as
you know, claimed the Marshall Islands with no opposition
save for a little whining on the part of those silly squint-
eyed Japanese. At the moment we are negotiating with
certain Samoan chiefs regarding the advantages of a German Samoa. It will be good for the natives. We Herren-
volk are sure to treat them better than the thieving French
treat their own Tahitians. But both the British and U.S.
navies seem unhappy at the thought of a German naval
base in those waters, and unlike the harmless Japs, they
can make trouble for us should we give them an excuse.''

"Blackbirding isn't a good enough excuse?''

"Goddamn it! Not one Samoan native has been forced
to work against his will for the German *government*! This
other business with the German-owned civilian firm is, I'll
admit to you frankly, not good for the business of coloniz-
ing cannibal isles for the sake of advancing civilization.
We are looking into Halle und Feldmacher's dealings; and
should we find they have been behaving badly, we shall
deal with the matter discreetly. And at their offices in
Bremerhaven! The last thing we want is a wild-west raid
on a South Pacific Island, no matter *who* is at fault! So,

again, how much do you and Verrier want to simply, how you say, butt out?''

Captain Gringo gazed wistfully at the door through his cigar smoke as he replied, ''You sure know how to tempt a girl. If you were anyone else, I'd take the money and run. But, yeah, we owe one another a certain officer's honor. So thanks, but no thanks. A deal is a deal, and we've already set the gears in motion. What happens now?''

Von Linderhoff sighed, got up, and opened a drawer to take out Captain Gringo's revolver. He handed it back to the now-recovered American, saying, ''I told you when you woke up this was a friendly visit. The *next* time, it may go harder with you, Herr Walker. It was not my wish to declare war, but if that is what you want, so be it.''

Captain Gringo put his gun away, saying, ''Thanks. You're on your own the next time I have you in my sights, too. But you sure have been acting sort of delicate for a guy who's already tried to kill the princess at least.''

Von Linderhoff frowned down at him and asked, ''What are you talking about? If I had ordered that big native girl executed, she'd be *dead* by now!''

''You know, I halfway believe you. But if *your* guys didn't toss that bomb . . . Never mind. Your guys were the ones who were trying to scare us off. I knew there had to be two bunches working at cross-purposes.''

He got to his feet and waited for the rug to stop spinning under him as Von Linderhoff growled, ''Always, Herr Gott, the man has to speak in riddles? What is all this nonsense about assassins and people trying to frighten you? Haven't you learned by now we Germans favor the *direct* approach?''

Captain Gringo picked up his hat, rubbed his head again ruefully, and said, ''That last move still feels pretty direct. But no shit, Von Linderhoff, wasn't it your guys who returned the dame's things after helping themselves to her checkbook and passport?''

''Don't be ridiculous. We have printers who can furnish our agents with any sort of checkbooks or passports they might feel the need for. My people are *spies*, not sneak thieves!''

''Hmm, maybe we *should* put our heads together, then. If you're not just bullshitting me in the line of duty, we seem to have *three* sides trying to keep us from rescuing those natives just off the coast. There's you with the clubs and gunboats; somebody playing spooky but so-far-harmless *tricks;* and some deadlier bastards playing for *keeps*! Okay, I know who you are. *One* of the other players is probably Halle und Feldmacher. Unless I see some labor contracts signed by the guys diving for pearls not far from here, I'm assuming they play rough. But who the fuck could the *third* side be?''

Von Linderhoff shrugged and said, ''You are right about us having a gunboat, and you have been *warned*: Others do not interest me unless they too try to get in my way.''

''Hit 'em once for me,'' said Captain Gringo as Von Linderhoff politely opened the door for him. Then, as he saw the door had never been locked, he nodded grudgingly and added, ''Okay, okay, have your pound of flesh. Thanks for not killing me when you had the chance.''

The sardonic German's voice was grim as he replied, ''Don't count on it a second time. We are even now. You have been *told*, not *asked*, to stay away from the Guardian Bank. If you persist in this madness, it may go hard with you.''

''It already has. You should see some of the crew we have aboard. Can I assume I'm safe from your agents here in Puntarenas for now?''

Von Linderhoff shrugged and answered, ''Here you

present no threat to my own mission. If you are wise, you will not put out to sea with your crazy Kanaka princess."

They'd made it to what seemed the front entrance of whatever this was. But Captain Gringo turned in the vestibule to say, "You seem to know a lot about her nibs and the place she comes from. While I have you in a chatty mood, is there any chance native politics could account for at least some of the skulduggery? That spooky stuff smells sort of witch doctor to me, if I buy your story that it can't be Black Forest Elves acting cute."

Von Linderhoff shrugged and said, "Princess Manukai doesn't have to worry about the kahunas of Konakona trying to frighten her. Her proud poppa is the high kahuna as well as king."

"You keep track? You even have German spies on Konakona?"

Von Linderhoff laughed in an oddly boyish manner, considering the saber scar, and asked, "What did you think the Lutheran minister there was, a *Russian* spy? We have been monitoring every move the silly girl has made since she got her poppa's permission to do whatever it is she thinks she is doing in a man's world."

"I believe you. But while we're on the subject, how come they sent a woman to do a man's work? I mean, I know she's pretty big, but just between us, she's not my idea of a proud Kanaka warrior!"

Von Linderhoff shrugged and said, "She's not. Her volunteering caused quite a scandal back on Konakona, as a matter of fact. Her younger brother and future co-heir refused to lead the expedition. I must say, for a naked savage, the young man showed surprisingly good sense, nicht wahr?"

They shook on it and parted friendly. Out on the deserted street once more, Captain Gringo peered back at the building he'd just left. A small brass plate by the door read,

"Halle und Feldmacher, Puntarenas, Bremerhaven." He grimaced and muttered, "I might have known."

The quaint custom of La Siesta began to make more sense as the deserted streets of Puntarenas turned to bake ovens. By one o'clock it was getting hot enough to wilt the cast-iron streetlamps, and the afternoon was early yet. But the Casa Real catered to foreigners who didn't know any better. So a doorman dressed as fancy as a Mexican general had to stand out front under the awning anyway.

The doorman stared thoughtfully at Captain Gringo as the big Yank joined him in the shade. The Americano was obviously too shabby to allow inside and obviously too big to argue with. Captain Gringo solved the problem by tipping generously as he explained that his friends El Señor y La Señora Verrier were expecting him. The doorman decided anyone so prosperous had to be respectable and directed him to inquire at the desk inside.

The lobby was a little cooler and a lot darker than the dazzling sunlight he'd come in from. As he stood near the entrance letting his eyes adjust, he heard a cobra hiss and spotted Gaston lurking in a grove of potted palms. The Frenchman led him to a corner settee and said, "The princess is asleep upstairs, thank God. If you want to awaken the sleeping beauty, she's in suite three-three-three. Here's your duplicate key. I took the liberty of having extra ones made at a locksmith's down the street."

Captain Gringo pocketed the key as he sat down, but said he'd pass on the charms of the princess right now. He said, "I hope you impressed it on her she's not to go out unescorted, for any reason?"

Gaston sighed and replied, "I repeated it every time she

gave me the chance. It is not easy to converse with a sex maniac, even when you meet one with a brain. The woman is a moron, Dick. Wait, I take that back. I don't think even a moron would have signed the hotel register with her right name before I could stop her! Fortunately, when one pays a week in advance, in gold, room clerks read poorly without their glasses. I paid for unlimited occupancy, by the way, in case we wish to stage an all-night orgy. May I suggest we stage one and then get our adorable asses *out* of here before someone blows them off?''

"Forget about Manukai and her suite for now. Have you had time to contact any of your adorable rogues, Gaston?"

"But of course, and that is why I say we should back off. The game is up. When I approached Sanchez to inquire about recruiting our own little army, he told me all the really fine thugs in Puntarenas were recruited days ago by the firm of Halle und Feldmacher, as what they called, most delicately, 'company security guards.' Business is business, to Sanchez. So I was able to get him to sell me the vital statistics. In addition to such guards as they must have already *had,* out on the Guardian Bank, they just recruited a hundred and sixty-four more! Sanchez says he might be able to scrape us up a dozen at the most, and he refuses to vouch for them being true professionals. So one might assume he is speaking of juvenile delinquents or fighting drunks at best.''

Captain Gringo grimaced and reached for a smoke as he asked, "How did you make out with the arms dealer?"

Gaston reached for his own claro as he replied, "Très half-ass. Garcia had only one Maxim and a très rusty Browning. He tried to sell us a rusty Hotchkiss as well that did not look to me as if it would shoot worth the shit, even cleaned. Why do you suppose they designed the Hotchkiss so très bizarre, Dick?"

"Easy. If you don't want to pay Maxim for his basic patent, you gotta design around it. Wait till you see how the German parabolic machine-gun action is supposed to work. Browning is the only outfit honest enough to just make a deal with the Maxim brothers and the hell with it. So the one you picked up ought to do, if it's not too fouled to put back in shape. When and where do we take delivery?"

"Garcia says he can bring them to the schooner under the cover of darkness as well as cordwood, COD, of course. But why are we discussing the tedious cleaning of used weaponry at all? Haven't you been paying attention? The blackbirders no doubt have their own automatique weapons, with an army to man them as well. If that is not enough to dampen your enthusiasm, may I point out once more that we don't even know *which island* out there we are supposed to be invading with a handful of unprofessional fighters aboard a thin-skinned schooner with not a single deck gun to call its own?"

Captain Gringo lit his claro, took a thoughtful drag on it, and said, "It gets worse. A German gunboat just dropped anchor in the harbor, and I just had a talk with our old Prussian pal, Von Linderhoff. He hinted that they mean to blow us out of the water before we ever get there, if we're dumb enough to try!"

"Merde alors, in that case what are we doing here? Are you waiting for the Kanakas to give us our front money before we scamper back to San Jose?"

"That would be dishonest," Captain Gringo said, adding, as he spotted what was coming through the hotel entrance, "Hmm, what have we here?"

Gaston muttered, "Room two-sixty-nine. The redhead wears a wedding band," as the two non-native girls approached the desk for their key. The redhead was red-headed indeed, and her companion's hair was so blond it was almost white. Both looked a little wilted from the heat outside, and their thin white cotton sportswear clung to them more than the designers might have intended. They'd obviously been in the tropics long enough to know better than to wear the usual corsets and unmentionables of the Gibson girl type. It usually took a white woman less than forty-eight hours to learn *that* down here, though. So they might or might not be old tropic hands. Whatever they were, they sure were yummy. The redhead had the bigger derriere and the blonde had the bigger tits. Captain Gringo chuckled and said, "Oh Lord, decisions, decisions."

But Gaston growled, "I'll take the one in the middle. The redhead is registered as a Frau Keller. The blonde signed in as one Fraulein Manheim, and they're both from Bremerhaven. Need I say more?"

"Glug. I just came from the local offices of Halle and Feldmacher here in town. Von Linderhoff's using it as his local front. I wonder if the dames work directly for him or just the company. Did they check in before or after you and Manukai, Gaston?"

The Frenchman smiled thinly and said, "Alas, they were residents of this hotel before we arrived. So they could hardly be following us. But they still keep sinister company, non?"

"Yeah. I wonder where they just were. There's not a hat shop or beauty parlor open in town right now. But I can't see even a pair of tourists just enjoying a walk around town in this heat."

The two German girls moved out of sight, and Gaston suggested, "Forget them. Halle und Feldmacher must have some office chores that need not be concerned with us. We were discussing how to get out of this mad business gracefully, non?"

"Non. Not until I know for sure it's hopeless. The princess can always get someone else to lay her, and the guys and gals on the schooner are no doubt better off not trying. But meanwhile, naked natives are working under the same hot sun outside, as slaves. Held on a barren, hot rock pile by an outfit that's beginning to steam my ass. That fucking Von Linderhoff manages to look down on the rest of the human race even when he's trying to be friendly. I wonder what it is about Prussians that makes it so easy to dislike them?''

Gaston wrinkled his nose in disgust and said, ''Had you been with me during the Franco-Prussian War, you would not have to ask. But look at the bright side, Dick. No matter how much the young kaiser wants to match the empire of his grandmother Victoria, he'll never be able to hold it. The Boche simply can't help acting like a très rude species of bully. So in the end, everyone else gangs up on him. The one thing an Irishman and Englishman or a Frenchman and a Russian can agree on is that a *German* can be a très disagreeable pain in the derriere. I think it may be all the sour food they eat, hein?''

Captain Gringo shrugged and said, ''Let's not worry about Kaiser Willy's plans for the future. Let's get back to those German blackbirders out on the Guardian Bank. The charts we have aboard the Orotiki aren't good for anything but ass-wiping. We need to find out what's really out there. That Kanaka kid was picked up by honest Costa Rican fishermen. Ergo, some of the local fishermen must know more about those waters than the guys who made dots on official charts. You're better at getting around the slums without attracting attention than I am. So see if you can find a native who knows what's going on out there, and where. If he's got a boat and wants to charter it for a moonlight cruise, so much the better.''

''Sacre bleu! Are you suggesting we invade a strongly held slave colony aboard a fishing lugger, you maniac?''

''Not really. But it's generally a good idea to scout the

enemy before you attack. With the princess here at the hotel and her schooner tied up waiting for her, and both no doubt under observation, nobody should pay all that much attention to a known native fishing boat as it puts out to catch squid or something. If you can find us one with a hairy-chested crew, and we take along at least the Maxim, just in case . . ."

"Just in case of what?" Gaston cut in, adding: "If we manage to sail discreetly close enough to pinpoint the exact island and we are not challenged by a German gunboat, we won't *need* any weaponry. If we are challenged while bobbing about in a glorified rowboat, no weaponry it could carry would do us any good against even one one-fifty-five; and the last Boche gunboat I observed in these waters carried more than one big gun!"

Captain Gringo nodded and said, "You must have seen the same one I just did. She's got turrets fore and aft. But she's not the only vessel we may run into off the Guardian Bank. Those blackbirders didn't kidnap pearl divers with a German gunboat. And some automatic fire at the waterline ought to slow down any thin-skinned schooners or power launches we run into. Meanwhile, as long as the Orotiki's tied up here in Puntarenas, that more serious German gunboat *has* to stay in port to keep an eye on *her,* see?"

"Eh bien, but can you say for sure they don't have a sister ship keeping its one-fifty-five eyes on the Guardian Bank's pearl beds, Dick?"

Captain Gringo shrugged and said, "Nothing but death and taxes are for *sure*. But if you'd like an educated guess, it's ten to one in our favor. The company just recruited civilian gun-slicks, meaning no German military out there so far. I'm not sure just what Der Kaiser has on his little pointed head about the Guardian Bank, but if Germany's pussyfooting in on Samoa delicately, an open grab in Central American waters seems unlikely. They're probably using the same approach us Yanks used in the Sandwich Islands, and that was so slow all the details haven't been settled yet. First you send in the missionaries, then the traders; then you get everyone dependent on you for heaven and hardware, subvert the ruling class, and fill all the new civil-service positions with your own kind until they're *really* running everything. One day you notice the quaint native rulers are just obstructing the progress of civilization, so you have to depose them for their own good and—''

"I know how it's done," Gaston cut in. "How did you think we French got Indo-Chine? But remember the Boche are not as delicate as the rest of us, Dick. When *they* decided it would be nice to civilize some East Africans, they simply shot down everyone who did not speak German and put the few survivors who learned German, fast, to work. Halle und Feldmacher could have recruited all the willing pearl divers they needed for much less than any white would work. But that does not seem to be the way Boche view free enterprise. As I keep repeating, if only you would listen, we are dealing with real suckers of cock, avec guns, and the only people we have to work with are happy-go-lucky hula dancers who may or may not know how to fight. If there is one thing I learned about the Boche in Seventy, at a place called Sedan, it is that the Boche fight as hard as they brag!''

Captain Gringo consulted his watch and said, "You'd better leave first. I'll tail you a couple of blocks to make sure you're not being shadowed. Then I'll head back to the schooner and wait for you with my sweaty duds off and my hard-on, if a lady I just met back there still likes me."

"Dick, you are being très cruel to animals!"

"I know. The sooner you finish your chores in town, the sooner you'll be able to join us. I'll ask old Likelike if she has a friend for you."

Gaston made a dreadful remark about Captain Gringo's mother and got wearily to his feet to leave. Captain Gringo waited a few moments, yawned, and got up to head for the public toilets across the lobby. As he did so, a pair of German agents who'd been hiding in another palmy corner behind yesterday's edition of *La Prenza* exchanged thoughtful glances. One said, "We had better follow the Frenchman. He can't be going out to buy flowers in the heat of La Siesta. So we'd better find out what he's *really* after, nicht wahr?"

The other spy asked, "What about the others, here in the hotel?" And the one in command said, "Ach, it's obvious nobody else will make any interesting moves until at least three. Not even that big Yankee is dumb enough to go out in this heat when he doesn't have to. So the little Frog must be up to something important. Come, let us follow before he can get out of sight. I certainly don't want to have to *run* after him in this hellish heat!"

They both rose, as Captain Gringo watched them from the slit of the toilet door. As they ambled innocently out, the junior spy squinted and said, "There he goes, around that corner to our south. But you are all too right about the heat, and Von Linderhoff told us to keep our eye on *pussy* for him!"

His boss growled, "What is there for a gentleman to report about sweaty pussy behind a locked door? Let Captain Gringo worry about it. If half of what they say about him is true, he'll still be screwing when we come back. After we find out what *Verrier* is up to."

Since Gaston was out of sight, the two burly Germans made no attempt to hide their actions as they simply moved across the calle to the shade on that side and followed it to the corner Gaston had rounded.

Captain Gringo waited and did the same—once the guys

tailing Gaston had peered around the corner, seen Gaston cutting around yet another, and followed.

.The game went on for six or seven zigzag blocks, since Gaston was a caution when it came to ducking around corners. Each time he did, the Germans would leg it after him while Captain Gringo waited for them to round a corner so he could follow the same route. It was hot as the hinges of hell, and the narrow shady streets smelled awful as Gaston worked them all deeper into a squalid part of town where even if someone looked out an unshuttered window during the afternoon heat, they never saw anything the *police* could get out of them. Gaston was, in fact, in an alleyway he knew well indeed when he decided to make his move.

The Germans, of course, saw him enter it. Their mistake was in following a knockaround old guy like Gaston into *any* alley. The agent in the lead took a cautious peek around the corner, cheek pressed to rough stucco, and said, "It's clear. He's moved through the block, the skittering little cockroach. Cover me. I'm moving down to the far end, schnell! We must not let him lose us, and it's beginning to look as if he's trying to!"

"Be careful!" his companion warned as the leader made tracks down the narrow alley. He didn't make it to the far end. As he passed a door-niche, Gaston stepped out, knife in hand, to end his curiosity forever with a well-placed stab in the back.

The agent covering the recently living back of his comrade of course gasped "Ach!" and drew his Mauser. But before he could nail Gaston, he gasped "Ach!" again and dropped it when Captain Gringo blew his spine in two with a well-aimed round of hot lead!

Gaston had his own .38 out as Captain Gringo rounded the corner on the double, leaping over the body blocking the alley entrance. Gaston held his fire after all as the taller

American joined him by the other body. The little Frenchman smiled up at him and said, "Bless you, my child. Let us get our adorable asses in gear before the très fatigue police arrive. Must you always be so *noisy*?"

Captain Gringo told him to hold the thought as he dropped to one knee to pat down the handiest corpse. He took out the dead man's passport and said, "German. It doesn't say right out he works for German Intelligence, but one out of two ain't bad. Which way do you suggest we run?"

Gaston said, "This way, of course," as, suiting deeds to words, he put his gun away, reached up with both hands, and boosted himself over a garden wall. Captain Gringo did the same. So, as they heard the distant melody of police whistles, they were strolling across a pleasant pateo toward the back of a house facing the street to the east. The back door opened and a lady wearing more paint than clothing stared out warily before she recognized Gaston of old and said, "Oh, it's you. Are you boys really *that* hard up? I know the front door's locked for La Siesta, but, no shit, the girls are really pretty tired and sweaty right now."

Gaston introduced Captain Gringo to the madam, by a ridiculous name, and said, "In that case, we may settle for a drink, Querida. Since I never lie to the ones I love, I must tell you frankly we climbed over your back wall to avoid trouble."

She said, "I heard a gunshot just now. Was that you, Gaston?"

"Mais non, on my mother's honor I can swear I have not fired my gun all day. But someone else must have. A pair of Anglo types lie casually about in the alley out back at the moment. We did not seek to determine the cause of their unusual positions. We, like yourself, find it très fatigue to discuss matters we know little about with La Policia, hein?"

The madam said, "Oh shit, let's all get inside before some nosy cop sticks his head over my back wall. Do I have your word you didn't shoot those tourists, Gaston? Sooner or later someone's going to ask me what I know about it, you know, and a girl like me has to stay in good with the authorities."

Gaston drew his revolver as she led them inside, saying, "Smell my weapon if you do not believe me. I am très hurt that you even suspect me of such unseemly behavior, Conchita mia! I already swore, on my mother's honor, I have not shot a single soul, today at least."

The madam laughed and said, "Put that gun away, you idiot. Your mother wouldn't have *had* you if she'd had any *honor*. But I have never caught you in a lie, so you must be either truthful or too clever a liar for La Policia to catch up with. I don't really care one way or the other, as long as me and my girls are not involved."

She led them into a darkened sitting room and waved them to seats as she poured drinks at a corner bar. Gaston nudged Captain Gringo and whispered, "Would you like some of that, Dick? It's too hot to fuck, but she gives très fantastique head!"

"I heard that," Conchita said as she turned with a tray of drinks. It didn't seem to have upset her to be described as a great blow-job, judging from her Mona Lisa smile as she swayed over to them, the front of her thin silk kimono open for full inspection. It opened wider as she sat across from them, saying, "He's full of shit. I don't service the customers myself, and Gaston knows it."

Gaston took his highball with a chuckle, saying, "True, she only fucks her friends, and she hasn't got an enemy in the world."

Captain Gringo joined the laughter as he took charge of his own drink. He knew what Gaston was up to, and it seemed to be working. Conchita didn't ask anything else

about the bodies out back as she defended herself from
Gaston's outrageous remarks. Captain Gringo thought she
might be getting really steamed when he noticed she was
crossing her legs and covering up with her kimono. So he
said, "I haven't believed anything he's told me about a
lady since he accused his own aunt of introducing him to
oral sex, Conchita. We both know he comes from a
disgraceful family, but he's just too ugly for incest."

Conchita laughed and said, "Oh, you've heard about
dear old Aunt Mimi, too? He's the only customer we've
ever had who can make even my tougher girls blush, and I
must say we get some pretty rough trade when the fishing
fleet's enjoyed a good catch!"

Captain Gringo brightened and asked, "Do you know
any fishermen who might like to make some real money
sort of rough, Conchita?"

The hard-boiled whore shrugged and said, "Quien sabe?
What kind of rough stuff are we talking about, and more
important, what's in it for me?"

Gaston was gently kicking Captain Gringo's booted
ankle for some reason. So the American said, "What we
need with a tough crew and a fast boat is of no concern to
a lady who likes to stay in good with La Policia. But
what's *in* it for you is a finder's fee, of course. Ten percent
of whatever we can work out with the fishermen?"

She shook her head and said, "Not good enough. I can't
tell muchachos who trust me to just *trust* me! Who but a
fool would even agree to meet with a stranger, not even a
Costa Rican, for to risk his ass and his boat doing what,
when, and with whom?"

Captain Gringo ignored Gaston's frantic foot as he
smiled thinly and said, "Bueno, you are too wise in the
ways of this wicked world to even attempt to fool, Conchita.
It's a gun-running deal. We want to run up the coast with a
few cases of Krags for the Nicaraguan rebels, and the

winning side's patrol boats are on to the usual tramp steamer we've been using up to now. Would you spread the word we're willing to pay well for some guys with a shallow-draft lugger and some knowledge of the reefs up that way?''

She shrugged and said, ''You'll have to pay well indeed, if anyone who screws here is mad enough to take such a chance! I'll spread the word, but don't hang by your thumbs waiting for to hear from me. By the way, where are you two to be found—on the outside chance I succeed in finding you a boatload of lunatics?''

Captain Gringo finished his drink, put it down, and stood up as he said casually, ''We'll check back with you. We were staying at another whorehouse up the slope, but we had to check out when the madam began to wonder why La Policia was strolling by so often.''

''Madre de Dios, you expect simple fishermen to join up with you when both the Nicaraguans and our own government seem to be on to you?''

Gaston rose too, saying in a soothing tone, ''Do your best, Querida. There is no great hurry. We shall drop by later in the week to see how you made out.''

She led them to her front entrance, muttering they were both nuts, and let them out, but barred her door firmly behind them. As they strolled innocently away, Gaston asked, ''What was all that shit of the bull about, Dick? Didn't you feel it when I signaled you to shut up?''

''Yeah, and remind me I owe *you* a black-and-blue ankle, too! But I'd already started before you warned me you only trusted her so far. So I had to keep talking, and as long as I was talking, I figured I may as well leave some red herrings for Von Linderhoff and the cops to sniff at.''

Gaston frowned thoughtfully and said, ''Eh bien, if the local police pick up rumors of some mysterious strangers planning to scoot up the coast towards Nicaragua, they may discount or simply be confused about leaks involving our true reasons for wishing to go fishing somewhere else. But surely Von Linderhoff would not be put off by such an obvious ruse, since he already knows we are interested in the Guardian Bank, to the west-southwest, non?''

"How are the Germans supposed to hear anything Conchita says, unless they sure like to screw sloppy? Even if a sailor off that gunboat picks up rumors along with the clap, there's nothing to the story I just fed her that connects *us* to that whorehouse. Where in the hell did you come up with a name like 'Gonner Swensen' for a Yank like me?''

"I served with a big blond species of Scandinavian answering to that name in the Legion one time. He was killed at Camerone by the Juaristas. I thought it better to have you described as a Viking than a Yank, and I don't even know whether Swensen was a Swede or Dane. Latins are even more confused by big blonds. So, should Conchita be less trustworthy than one hopes, let us hope we confused her beaucoup, hein?''

Captain Gringo said that sounded fair. So when they came to a main cross street, still deserted because of La Siesta, they split up. Gaston went on to see if he could do some recruiting among crooks he really trusted, and Captain Gringo followed the calle over to the waterfront to go back aboard the Orotiki.

He didn't know if they had a word for La Siesta in Kanaka. But with the tar bubbling up between the sun-toasted planks of the schooner's decking, the people aboard had caught on to local custom fast, and there was not a soul in sight. He thought that seemed a hell of a good idea, himself. But he had a last look around before going below.

Out on the harbor, the German gunboat lay at anchor, broiling in the sun and probably a steel-walled brick-kiln inside as well. Even the harbor gulls were holed up for La Siesta now as the tropic sun glared down from, say, two-thirty. So Captain Gringo was more than a little surprised to see two white-clad feminine figures hurrying his way along the hot cobbles of the quay under parasols that couldn't really be helping either the red or blond head they were attempting to shade. They were obviously making for the Orotiki. The redhead, in fact, was waving up at him now. He moved to the gangplank to see what they had in mind, aside from sunstroke.

As they both came aboard, the blonde in the lead said, "Ach, Captain Gringo, so gut is it to find you here! Mein sister, Alfrieda here, would like a word mitt you. Only she does not Englisch speak, so I, Hilda, must for her translate, ja?"

"Not under this hot sun," he replied, leading them both to the hatchway leading under the quarterdeck and sliding it open for them. Inside, it was still too damned hot, but a lot cooler. He said, "I'm not sure which of these staterooms is supposed to be mine. But one of them must be. Let's see."

He passed the entrance to Kuruhai's cabin, ignoring the snores he heard coming from it, and tried the next one. Both German girls gasped, and he said, "Ooops, sorry," as he quickly slid the vented paneling shut again for the startled couple they'd caught in the act of a so-called crime against nature. It was obviously too hot for even a Kanaka to just plain screw.

He tried the other side of the gangway, opened up an imposing stateroom that didn't seem to be occupied—judging from the fresh linens on the bunk—and said, "This is either mine or the boss lady's, and she's at the hotel, so what the hell. Come in and make yourself comfortable, girls. I'll see if there's anything to refresh ourselves with in this cabinet."

There was. He knew now it was Manukai's layout, as he exposed some very expensive booze to view. He suggested gin and tonic, in this heat, and both his mysterious pretty visitors agreed as they flopped down on the bunk looking wilted. He didn't think he'd better suggest they unbutton their high-collar bodices just yet. But as soon as he'd handed them their refreshments, he tossed his hat aside and removed his jacket. The redhead stared soberly at his exposed shoulder holster and said something in German to the blonde, who said, "Mein sister wants to know if it is true you are very tough, and that you will shoot anyone for money."

He found a stool under the liquor cabinet and hauled it out to perch on before he said, "I'm a soldier of fortune, not a hired assassin. But just who did you ladies have in mind?"

Hilda said, "Der manager here, of Halle und Feldmacher. He ist a fiend from hell!"

"No kidding? Funny you should mention that. You girls are not alone in your opinion. But what on earth has Halle und Feldmacher ever done to *you*? No offense, but you two certainly don't look like pearl divers!"

The blonde looked as if she was about to burst into tears as she said, "Please nicht to mock us, and if you don't mind, your Englisch please keep zimpler. Mein sister, Die Frau Keller, a stockholder in Halle und Feldmacher ist. The shares were left to her by mein late brother-in-law, a director of the company. He died last year, they told her, of a fever caught in das South Pacific on a trading expedition. But a few months ago, a crewman who aboard his trading schooner back in Bremerhaven arrived, to tell mein sister her man had by a native been with a spear stabbed instead!"

Captain Gringo nodded soberly and said, "That *would* make most widows wonder, wouldn't it? But how come you girls came here to Central America to check the story out?''

The two of them chatted in German a moment. Then, with the redhead up-to-date again, the blonde explained, "We went first to a place called Konakona, between Samoa and Tahiti, where mein sister's husband lies buried in a Lutheran churchyard. Der missionary was not able to tell us all that happened. He said Alfrieda's husband had died on a smaller island a day or more to sail away, und so, by the time they brought the body to Konakona, in a lead-foil-wrapped sea chest, he wise thought it nicht to open it. We asked the government there for help. But the government of Konakona brown laughing savages ist, und, while they were polite enough, they could not tell us just what happened to her Hansel. Aber, some of the natives able were to tell us that other company men who had with her husband been when he died were now pearling off der Guardian Bank. . . . Ist Guardian Bank feminine or masculine in Englisch?''

"Never mind. Call 'em die, der, or rocks. Have you girls been *to* the Guardian Bank?''

The blonde shuddered and said, "Ja, and it was grässlich! So slim the poor natives were, mitt whip marks all over their brown skins! They are working them like beasts, und beating them when they don't come to the surface mitt pearls. But even we know there can't be a pearl in every oyster. So why hit a poor frightened boy who ist only his best trying?''

"We heard the captive divers are being mistreated,'' he cut in, going on to demand: "How did you girls get out there, and more important, how did you get safely *back*?''

They consulted each other in German, probably to keep Alfrieda from wetting her pants as she tried to follow the conversation she obviously found more important than understandable. Then Hilda said, "We arrived here unannounced. So they could not stop us when we simply hired a Costa Rican yacht to sail out there. Once we there were, the company men to stop us from around looking tried. But it ist a small island, und we are more determined womens than we may appear. I don't think we saw everything. They tried to up cover by having the natives run away when we tried to speak to them. They have them trained, I think, like dogs. By the time we decided we had better leave, the situation ugly was becoming. But the crew of our Costa Rican yacht also tough looking was, und more than one of them told the men out there what they thought of them. So we left before a fight could start. Und naturlich, we reported conditions out there at once to the German consulate here in Puntarenas!''

"What did they say? That they'd look into it, and that meanwhile the two of you should just go on back to Bremerhaven?''

"Ach, have *you* spoken to our consulate, too, Captain Gringo?''

"Call me Dick. I don't have to speak to consuls in banana ports. They all say the same things, and none of them really have any power. You girls are going to hate me for saying this, but he gave you good advice.''

"But we don't wish back to Germany to go, now that we know what ist going on in the name of Halle und Feldmacher! It ist not just that mein sister stock holds in it, or that her man died working for it. What they are *doing* out there is a disgrace to the name of Der Vaterland, und we are both the daughters of a Prussian Oburst!''

He said, "Hold the thought,'' as he rose and ducked out a minute. He went to the skipper's cabin and got a pencil as well as the admiralty chart without waking Kuruhai. He brought it back to the German girls and asked, "Could you ladies pinpoint the exact island we're talking about?''

They had to think about that in German awhile. Then,

when they had it narrowed down, they were both only somewhere near the spot Kuruhai had stabbed with his bigger finger. Hilda said, "So much alike these dots all look! From the bow of a boat ist easier. The surf a way of splashing over the smaller rocks und submerged reefs has. Also, the tin roofing of the company compound ist not hard to see from even far away. We could *guide* you there, we think, but all we can tell from this map is that the right island would be here, or *here,* about."

He grimaced and said, "I could use a guide, Hilda. But you don't look like you could use a bullet in your pretty blond skull. So we'll have to work out something safer. How do I go about contacting the crew of that first yacht you chartered? They sound like decent guys, and they must know the way even better than you if they took you out there."

Hilda fired full-automatic in German at the redhead, who kept nodding or shaking her head and shooting back just as fast. It was no wonder so many Germans went around acting tough. It was a hell of a language to say nice things in, judging from the way even two pretty girls seemed to gargle and snort in it. He'd read somewhere that North German was more guttural than South German or Austrian. So these otherwise attractive sisters had to come from as far north as Germany went.

When they'd finished calling the hogs, Hilda told him, "The address we did not think to write down. We by the depot asked where we a boat could charter, und a man there sent the captain to our hotel. Perhaps if we just ask around town again—"

He stopped her with a disgusted snort and said, "I don't know what it is about you dames. You all seem to think the way to get away with something sneaky is to ask all over town when you want to hire a sneak! My pal, Gaston, might be able to find us a skipper who knows his way around the Guardian Bank. If he can't, we just may have to let you tag along."

Hilda screamed with delight, leaped to her feet, and came over to give him a big wet kiss. Not to be left out, the redhead followed and kissed him on the rise.

He laughed and said, "Down, girls. It's not settled yet. The first thing we have to worry about now is getting you both ashore and under cover. If you were seen coming aboard, we want to let them think you're still aboard while we hide you somewhere else."

He pried himself loose from the giggling sisters and moved over to a built-in wardrobe as Hilda said, "I do not understand. Why should anyone be the two of us harmless women watching, Dick?"

"You have to ask, after you've seen and been seen at a slave camp?" He sighed as he slid open Manukai's wardrobe. Half the dresses hanging in it were proper Victorian costumes, though big enough for both German girls to get into at once. He took a pair of flowery flowing mumus from their hangers and said, "Right. Try these on. They're sure to drag on the floor, but that's what pocketknives were made for, and we'll want to cover your hair with scarves anyway."

Hilda still seemed confused as she translated, and Captain Gringo could follow the drift of Alfrieda's reply enough to understand that she didn't understand either. But apparently they were good sports. So, giggling and blushing becomingly, they proceeded to peel off their white linen. He had a better idea of why they were so embarrassed when he couldn't help noting that neither had gone out in this heat wearing underwear. As he saw they'd both gotten their hair coloring, on their heads, from bottles, he started to ask why they couldn't have just slipped the mumus on over their own dresses. But as they slid the smooth silk print quickly down over the twin V's of brown pubic hair, he nodded and said, "Right, it would have been asking for heatstroke. But, Jesus, you might have *warned* me!"

Hilda laughed, sort of suggestively, as she smoothed her new, mostly red mumu over her heroic tits and said, "Ach, so naked I still feel, und also ist almost a meter too long for me, nicht wahr?"

The redhead in the mostly blue mumu seemed to be bitching about her own hem-length. So Captain Gringo dropped to one knee, got out his blade, and went to work. In the stuffy heat, he tried to ignore the musky odor they were both starting to give off at about the level of his nose as he knelt in front of them in turn. He muttered, "It's a good thing it's too hot and I already had some today."

"What did you say, Dick?" asked Hilda. So he answered, "Nothing. We have to move fast, while La Siesta is still working in our favor."

He rose to hand each a wide strip of floral silk, switching the colors for them as he said, "Okay, wrap these around your heads so not a lock of your hair shows. You're both way the hell too white to pass for Kanaka girls up close. But maybe at a distance, if you shade your faces and bare arms with your parasols and move straight across the quay."

"What about our own dresses, Dick? Shall we them carry mitt uns?"

"No. Take your purses, of course. But I may be able to recruit some vahines to stroll off and get lost wearing your familiar duds. I'm sort of playing this shell game by ear."

"But such a crazy game it ist!" Hilda sighed and said, "Why are we up like hula-hula girls gedressed, und what happens now?"

He opened a built-in desk, found paper and pencil, and wrote Mamma Rosa's address down as he said, "Now you both beeline for this posada and sit tight until we come for you. By now it's the one place in town the other side should have given up on. They know that we knew they were watching the place when we lit out for the same hotel you two have been staying at. So Mamma Rosa's should be the last place they'd expect any of us to go back to, see?''

"Dick, I see *nothing*! Who ist this *they* you speak of? Why must mein sister und mich from them hide?''

He said, "Just do as I say, or we won't let you play. If I don't send for you by, say, nine this evening, you'll know we recruited more sensible guides and your worries are over. Or at least they'll be over if you just go back to the hotel, check out, and head back to Germany. Tougher people will take over for you cute little things, and meanwhile, you already know too much about Halle und Feldmacher for your own good. So be careful. Let's go."

He led the disguised German girls out on deck. It felt as though the three of them had just stepped into a furnace. Hilda stared shoreward through the shimmering heat waves and said, "I see nobody at us staring, Dick." So he said, "You're not supposed to. They'll have a bitch making you out in this sunny shimmer, too. See that slot in the waterfront buildings to the left of that green awning? The calle it leads to leads to Mamma Rosa's. So get going!''

They discussed the matter in German. Then both kissed him on either cheek and moved down the gangplank, shapeless and nondescript under the shade of their parasols. He had to wait on deck until they were out of sight. It damned near killed him. As they vanished in the inky shadows across the way, he dashed back inside. He returned to Manukai's quarters, stripped to the buff, and poured himself a stiff drink. Then he pulled the counterpane off the bunk and flopped naked onto the white sheets. They were pure silk. It figured. It was so hot the bedding still felt like sandpaper on his flushed skin. As he got some liquid down, he raised one arm and noticed how red it was under his healthier tan. He nodded and muttered, "Yeah, you've been flirting with heatstroke for sure, you jerk-off. The natives knew what they were doing when they invented La Siesta."

But as he lazed on the bunk sipping gin and tonic in the stuffy shade, he began to feel better and knew he'd nipped the threat of heatstroke in the bud when, as his temperature dropped closer to normal, his dry red skin broke out in healthy sweat again.

Before he could really sweat up the bedding, things got even better. Outside, there was a crackle of lightning that made his hair tingle. Then someone upstairs pulled the plug and it began to rain fire and salt. He didn't get up to close the porthole over the bunk. Only a few drops were coming in, and they felt just great. He wondered if the German girls had made it to the posada before the storm broke. They probably wouldn't care if they were still outside. But the picture of those silk mumus plastered wet against those two great little bodies inspired another symptom of restored health. He chuckled fondly down at his dawning erection and growled, "Cut that out. There's no sense showing off when we're alone, old Organ Grinder."

Then the door slid open and Captain Gringo quickly covered his hard-on with his free hand as a lady he'd never been formally introduced to slipped in and slid the door shut after her.

She was a short, pleasantly plump vahine wearing flowers in her hair and little else. She had a tapa cloth draped around her ample hula hips, but her melonous breasts were bare as well as brown. She said, "Me called Atanua. Me friend of Likelike. She no speak Haole. So she send me to talky-talky you, bad boy."

He sat up straighter, pulling a corner of the top sheet across his lap as he asked her what Likelike wanted. His throbbing pecker certainly knew what *it* wanted right now.

But Atanua said, "Likelike say you makem nukinuki with her even though she vahine kine akamai belong along first mate! She say she try to tellem, but you make nukinuki along her anyway! Whassamatter you? You wanna big fight along big mate?"

He sighed and said, "Not if I don't have to! Does the mate know about my, ah, misreading a lady's intent?"

"For sure not! You crazy? You think Likelike wanna hit alongside head? She tellem me to tellem you not to make nukinuki along her no more. Okay, Sailor?"

He laughed and said, "I know enough to quit while I'm ahead, and I want you to tell her I'm really sorry. I thought she *wanted* to make love. She sure acted like she did. Don't you girls know enough to shake your heads, even if you don't speak English?"

Atanua shook her head and said, "You no savvy Kanaka ways my word. Suppose man grab vahine for make nukinuki, she not supposed to *fightem*. Vahines *smaller* than men. You not see this?"

"I'm beginning to, even though I know one vahine who doesn't fit the picture. You're saying it's up to the guy to *know* if a dame is going steady with another guy already. But how the hell's he supposed to know if she can't *tell* him?"

Atanua raised a hand to one of the flowers in her hair as she said, "Likelike tell you. She wearem blossom on this sideum hair. That mean she *gottem* lover. Suppose she *lookum* for lover, she wearem flower along *this* side, savvy?"

He nodded and said, "That's not too tough to remember. But what about a vahine wearing flowers on both sides, like you?"

"Oh, that mean she gottem lover but lookum for more lover. Me just love to make nukinuki along *everybody*!"

He laughed and said, "Welcome to the club." So

Atanua, who seemed to take things literally as well as
simply, dropped her tapa cloth and got on the bunk with
him, stark naked, as she calmly said, "Goodem. Likelike
say you one hellava fuck even whenna vahine don't wanna!"

He assumed she wasn't the latter as she plastered her
brown body against his and proceeded to chew his ear and
jerk him off at the same time. So he laughed, said, "Hey,
waste not, want not!" and rolled atop her to put his excited
shaft to better use for both of them. As he entered her, she
gasped, "Oh, Mamma Kapo! Thank you and other oramatua
belong Raki for this pretty Haole boy!"

Captain Gringo felt sort of grateful to her gods, or at
least their moral code, as he pounded her to glory with her
soft, plump limbs wrapped tightly around him while she
sent him hula messages with her brown bouncing hips. But
because her friend, the shy Likelike, had seen him first—
not all that long ago—and had given him one hell of a hula
lesson no matter what she said now, he wasn't able to
come in Atanua as quickly as most men would have had
to. She didn't seem to mind at all. The hot little vahine
climaxed almost at once, and then, when she saw he still
meant business, proceeded to croon Polynesian love words
into his ear as she softly chewed it, screwing hard.

But all good things must come in the end, so after he'd
come—with her, this time—they remembered how stuffy
the cabin was, even with the rain outside improving things
by the minute, and stopped for a smoke and their second
winds. She lay beside him, blowing smoke rings when it
was her turn on the claro and talking a mile a minute when
it wasn't. He was beginning to understand her Island
pidgin better as he got used to it, and some of the Kanaka
customs she explained to him were interesting. He kept
asking questions, partly to keep from having to lay her
again so soon, and mostly to try to save his ass from future
misunderstandings. It turned out her people weren't exact-

ly the carefree sex maniacs that white visitors assumed. The advantage of visiting the islands as a Haole, or non-person, was that no tapu could possibly apply to a *stranger.* So there was an open season on screwing whalers, missionaries, and such. But among *themselves,* the rules were so complicated it was small wonder they tended to go as nutty as a married Victorian in a whorehouse when all bets were off.

Aside from the obvious rule, not really a tapu, about leaving the steady vahine of another gent alone, the atuas and oramatua, or gods and spirits, got mad as hell at people who even bent one of the numerous tapus decreed by the kahunas, or priests. It wasn't as easy to get laid back on Konakona as he'd assumed. He was glad he didn't have to remember Atanua's moral code, save for how it might apply here on the schooner, because a lot of the tapus didn't make much sense, and worse yet, weren't consistent. When he thought he'd tripped her up on a rule that said nobody could even watch the king eat, but that he screwed girls from commoner families like a mink, she said, "Goddam, you not *listening,* Dick. Royal-family tapu tapu *mosta* time. Suppose common guy let his shadow fall on member of royal clan, he gotta killem self. But on feast day of Kapo, goddess of Fuck, all tapus off for day, and it great honor to make nukinuki with royalty, see?"

"If you say so. Your skipper, Kuruhai, says he's not allowed to make love to any of you girls on board because he's royal. How do you work out the shadows?"

She snuggled closer and explained, "Kahunas take off *some* tapus for special mission. But not nukinuki with commoner vahines. Thassaright. He gottem Manukai, suppose he wanna fuck."

"Wait a minute. He said he can't make love to his cousin, the princess."

She shrugged a bare shoulder against him and said, "Maybe so. Me no savvy all tapus belong along royal clan. Different spirits. Maybe she not allowed to make nukinuki with anybody but her blalah, the crown prince. Royal clan very snooty when it not Mamma Kapo's day. Back on Konakona, neither skipper or princess ever talk on people asame me, see?"

"I don't see at all! Are you saying brother-sister incest is *not* tapu?"

"Oh, *big* tapu, belong along gettem banged by thunder-bolt of Tangaroa suppose boy fuckem sister, if they *commoners*! But gods tell royalty to act different from common Kanaka made of shit. Suppose queen have baby with man of lower rank. What kinda prince would that be? Royal clan made from *blood* of gods, not *shit* of gods. So half-common baby would be *mess*! Better for royal vahine makeum babies with royal blalah, see?"

He grimaced and said, "Sort of. The ancient Egyptians had the same ideas about keeping blue blood pure. That's why Cleopatra had to marry her kid brother before she met a Haole named Julius. I guess it makes sense, when you study it some. The royal families of Europe are so inbred they're starting to produce moronic twits and toothy dames too ugly for anyone else to marry. But I think anything closer than a first cousin is tapu on the island of Great Britain. Let me ask you something else about your own island customs—"

But he didn't get to. For the door flew open and the skipper stared down at them from the doorway, demanding, "Hey, Haole, what the fuck you doing in Manukai's bunk?"

Captain Gringo said, "That's a pretty stupid question, Kuruhai. Relax, the princess is still at the hotel, in case the natives all look alike to you."

"Goddamit, Blalah, I don't care who you make nukinuki

with in your own quarters. But this ain't them! You and the Frenchman got smaller cabins down the companionway. Come on, I'll show you to 'em. Bring your vahine along if you want. But for god's sake, don't fuck her no more on the *royal sheets*!''

Captain Gringo and the girl got dressed—it was a lot easier for her—and followed the big Kanaka to the cabin assigned to him. He was glad, when he saw how small it was, that he'd cooled off in the bigger one. Atanua whipped off her tapa cloth and plopped down on the smaller bunk as the skipper turned away with a disgusted look. Captain Gringo told her to hold the thought and followed Kuruhai outside, saying, "Wait, we have things to worry about besides Manukai's bedding.''

"I'm not about to tell her,'' growled Kuruhai, adding, "She'd want to change quarters if she thought tapu ass had made nukinuki in that bunk; and you may have noticed, she needs a wide bunk and that's the only one we *got* for her! I suppose you poked around in her sea chest too, huh?''

"No. You can count her coins if you don't believe me.''

"Okay, ain't no big thing now that you know the rules, Haole. It's a good thing I didn't catch you with *Likelike*! My mate thinks she's his vahine kine akamai, and he don't like Haoles to begin with!''

"I'll stay clear of them both, then. I just sent Gaston to see if he can recruit us a fishing skipper who knows these waters better. Meanwhile, we're expecting a couple of machine guns and a lot of ammo after sunset. We're, ah, going to have to pay out some dinero. I mean big dinero.''

Kuruhai shrugged and said, "Ain't no big thing. You can dig in *my* sea chest all you want. The king said it was to spend on getting his people back. Come on, I'll load you up with some gold.''

They went to the skipper's own cabin, and he did.

Captain Gringo didn't think it might be delicate to mention that, despite the promises of the princess, neither he nor Gaston had been paid their front money yet. It was just as easy to pick up a few extra coins. The big Kanaka didn't seem to understand, or care, that a small gold Yankee Double Eagle was worth a good twenty bucks, or that a modest fistful added up to hundreds. The big Yank waited for the skipper to tell him to stop as he loaded both side pockets of his jacket. But Kuruhai didn't. So Captain Gringo just had to stop when both pockets were full.

When he'd done so, he grinned, took out fresh smokes, and handed one to the skipper, saying, "Well, whatever your game is, you're not in it for the money."

"What's that crack supposed to mean, Blalah?"

"I'm not sure. Tell me some more about this crown prince of yours back on Konakona. He's supposed to be Manukai's co-heir, right?"

Kuruhai lit his own claro, puffed on it as if it tasted disgusting, and said, "There's not much to tell. Prince Tinirau is a weakling, and we think he likes boys better than girls. He wouldn't *be* the co-heir if he was a real *man*. But our king knows he'll never be able to rule by himself. He even had to send his daughter, Manukai, on this mission!"

"So I've noticed. How come he couldn't just send *you*, Kuruhai? With all due respect to her nibs, she may be as tough, but she's not as bright as you."

Kuruhai shrugged and said, "That's why they sent me along to keep her from getting killed. It's a *face* deal, Blalah. Somebody from the king's close kin gotta straighten out them blackbirders. Old King Kamamamoku didn't *want* to send his favorite child. But what was he to do when his oldest son squats down to piss?"

"Queen Victoria's having trouble with a son who likes to play with dolls called Lillie Langtry, too. Princess

Manukai's probably tougher than *him,* as well. But has it occurred to either of you that if something happened to her chasing blackbirders, your sissy crown prince would have a solo shot at his old daddy's crown?''

The skipper nodded grimly and said, ''That's why the royal clan picked me to get her here and back, and why I picked nothing but commoners from nowhere near the royal court circles to crew the schooner. Ain't no way to have no palace coups aboard *Orotiki,* Blalah. So we only have to worry about them Haole blackbirders, right?''

''I'm not sure. Those guys who tried to blow Manukai out of bed up in San Jose didn't get to tell me exactly who they were or who sent them.''

''Yeah, but they was Costa Ricans, right?''

''Quien sabe? They had brown skins and black hair. After that it gets sort of iffy. Anyone can put on native costume. I do it all the time.''

''Oh shit, are you saying other Kanakas, from back home, could be out to hurt Manukai?''

''Whoever they were, they weren't trying to *hurt* her. They were trying to blast her through the ceiling, and they came mighty close to doing it. But you're not missing any of your original crew, are you?''

''Hell no; and besides, the princess would have said something if she'd known the guys who tried to kill her.''

''She might have, had she ever *seen* them. But she never did. We got her out of there poco tiempo, assuming they'd been mestizos. For all we know, they might have been. A sneaky German I know hires on ability. But we have to keep that palace political angle in mind. It might explain why we have too many fingers in this pie. We know which side *we're* on. We know the blackbirders work for Halle und Feldmacher and that they seem to have the backing of German Intelligence as well. So that makes one enemy side. With one *other* bunch of sneaks left over!''

Kuruhai looked puzzled. So Captain Gringo said, ''That's right. You weren't there when a lot of spooky stuff was going on. One spook seems out to kill while another plays a more delicate game with spooky but non-lethal stunts. I know you're not going to like this, but since the square-heads have had me and at least two nosy German girls at their mercy and, so far, we're all still breathing, I'd say they don't want to kill anybody unless they have to. That leaves someone else who doesn't give a shit about annoying the Costa Rican government.''

The big Kanaka scowled and demanded, ''What do you think those Germans are doing to our pearl divers out on the Guardian Bank, damn it?''

Captain Gringo explained. ''Treating them shitty as hell, maybe even killing them if they don't meet their quota. But those offshore islands aren't policed by Costa Rica. Costa Rica *is*! The German firm doesn't want to lose its trading privileges here, and you may have noticed that German gunboat finds Puntarenas a handy harbor with the hurricane season coming up not too far in the future. That's the only reason my old pal Von Linderhoff could have let me go with a lecture instead of some lead in my head. It's probably why they haven't spanked a couple of nosy tourist girls, too. So, yeah, we've got some no-bullshit killers left over.''

The skipper nodded soberly and growled, ''I'd better get the princess back aboard.''

''She's safe enough at the hotel. Probably asleep, now that La Siesta is about over. Have you ever noticed she seems to have a will of her own?''

Kuruhai opened a desk drawer and hauled out a man-size Mauser pistol as he insisted, ''Not as safe as she'll be on board, goddamn it!''

"But once anyone spots her boarding this schooner, they'll expect us to put out to sea, Kuruhai!"

"Ain't no big thing, Blalah. If you ain't ready to go after them fucking blackbirders, *I* am! I'm tired of all this Haole bullshit. The way you kill an enemy is to just go find the motherfucker and get it over with!"

They were still arguing about it as Captain Gringo followed the big stubborn skipper down the companionway. Kuruhai bellowed in Kanaka, and then a fat young guy wearing a first mate's cap stuck his head out and yelled at him in the same language for a while. Then, as the mate saluted casually, Kuruhai told Captain Gringo, "Makomotu here is in command till I get back with the princess. You can't talk to him, because he don't savvy Haole. But stay 'way from his vahine kine akamai, Likelike, and you'll get along with him okay till I take charge again."

Captain Gringo smiled innocently at Makomotu, who simply smiled back sort of bewildered. Captain Gringo felt awkward, so he told them both to keep up the good work and went back to his own cabin to see if his own vahine still loved him.

Apparently she did. So a short while later, Atanua was on top when the doorway of the smaller cabin slid open and Gaston said, "Eh bien, they told me I'd find you here. Has she got a friend who admires older men?"

Atanua was embarrassed enough to giggle and roll off. So Captain Gringo sat up and said, "Never mind all that. It's getting late. How did you do with that fishing boat?"

Gaston said, "It's a two-masted lugger, decked forward the mainmast, avec a très fishy-smelling open cockpit aft. I told them to slip up against our starboard side just after sundown."

"You told 'em right. They should be invisible from shore and screened by the schooner's bigger bulk from seaward as we pile aboard. Are you sure we'll have the machine guns by then as well?''

''Mais non, nothing involving skulduggery is ever a sure thing. But the Maxim should be here about the same time. That is not the main problem, Dick. The rogues I recruited are willing to take us anywhere in their stinky species of boat. But they don't *know* the Guardian Bank! The Costa Rican skipper says he has always tried to *avoid* them up to now. Something about sharks and uncharted reefs.''

Captain Gringo said, ''Shit!'' and swung his feet to the floor to haul his pants and boots on as the vahine cursed them both in her own lingo. The tall Yank stood up, strapped his gun rig on over his bare chest, and told Gaston, ''We may have some guides. But not unless we can take some heavy firepower along as well. Let's go below and see about some Krags for all hands, at least. How many people are we talking about?''

As they went out, Gaston explained there were a dozen Costa Rican fishermen, all trusted by their skipper, whom *Gaston* knew and trusted. But, such weapons as they had between them consisted mostly of machetes and antique pistols more suitable for killing sharks than the hired gun-slicks one might encounter among the keys of the Guardian Bank.

Captain Gringo found a ladderway down to the hold and Gaston followed. It was naturally black as a bitch down there until Captain Gringo struck a match, found a hanging lantern, and lit it. The dim light wasn't as much an improvement as they'd hoped. All the cargo was securely lashed in place, of course, but Kanaka notions of order must have called for placing beans near rifle ammo, with the rifles nowhere in sight. Captain Gringo unhooked the lantern and moved forward between the stacks, muttering,

"Come on. They probably have the Krags filed under 'K,' for coconuts."

Actually, they found one case of rifles under cases of canned pineapple and a barrel of rum. As Captain Gringo manhandled it out in the aisle and knelt to jimmy it open with his knife, Gaston sniffed and said, "Do you smell something très mysterious, Dick?"

"There's no mystery. Her name's Atanua, and *you* could use a bath right now, too. Today was really a scorcher."

Gaston wedged himself out of sight between two bales as he insisted, "Mais non, I do not smell anything as lovable as pussy or even sweat. I smell the old familiar reek of burning gunpowder. It is a scent no old soldier ever forgets, hein?"

Captain Gringo looked up, sniffed, and said, "Jesus, you're right! But who could have been firing a gun down here in the hold?"

Gaston's voice was firm, despite the way his heart was pounding, as he said simply, "Dick, run!"

But Captain Gringo moved to join him instead, of course, and it was a good thing Gaston was so small. Nobody Captain Gringo's size could have wedged himself between the steel hull and the bales from this angle as the old Frenchman kept moving toward the sputtering red eye of death in the form of a lit fuse glowing in the dark!

Captain Gringo just had time to spot it over Gaston's shoulder and gasp before the little Frenchman's strong hand had it snapped off and in his mouth. Gaston sizzled his tongue, spat, and said, "The taste leaves much to be desired, but the bouquet was très unusual. Regard that amusing streak of powder burn leading down that ship's rib from above. Some species of cochon planned this well in advance and simply had to light one end from up on deck! Let us see what the remaining fuse leads to, hein?"

They moved bales and boxes out of the way, then whistled as one when they found the dynamite, a lot of dynamite, fused to blow Orotiki and all aboard to kingdom come!

Captain Gringo growled, "Time for a roll call!" as he headed for the ladder, getting more pissed by the minute as his first numb surprise faded. He got Atanua dressed, sort of, to translate. Then he pounded on the mate's door and had her tell him to get everyone out on deck, on the double.

A few minutes later, everyone was. Or everyone was supposed to be. The mate explained, through Atanua, that aside from the skipper who'd gone ashore to get the princess, they seemed to be missing the Chinese cook.

Captain Gringo asked the vahine how come they'd had a Chinese cook in the first place, and she explained, "Oh Dick, everybody knows it take a Haole to cook Haole food. We hadda bring canned goods along 'cause poi don't keep good this long. Whassamatter you? You don't like Chinee cooking?"

"Chop suey ain't bad. But someone just tried to make a tossed salad out of us all just now." He explained for her to translate; and once she had, the mate started war-dancing around in a little circle, shouting awful things about squint-eyed Haoles in his own lingo, apparently. The vahine said, "Makomotu say he never meet a Chinee who wasn't motherfucker. He say it serve us right for taking him aboard at last minute without knowing his mamma and poppa. We go look for him now, no?"

"No. If it was your cook, he's long gone. They'd have told him where to run for after he lit the fuse. They'd have had to. How many guys are about to stay aboard a vessel about to go through the roof?"

Likelike, who'd been watching and listening from a discreet distance, suddenly pointed and called out. Captain

Gringo turned to see the princess and the skipper coming along the quay with a Costa Rican carrying her luggage from the hotel. They looked up, puzzled, and the skipper ran up the gangplank ahead of Manukai, gun drawn, to ask what the hell was up.

Captain Gringo said, "This schooner, almost. The timing is getting a little slicker now." He turned to Gaston and asked, "How much time was left on that fuse when we found it, Gaston?"

Gaston nodded and said, "Oui, just about enough to be detonating the dynamite right about *now*!"

Princess Manukai came aboard, fanning herself with a straw hat that would have looked sillier atop her big head, and demanded, "Would someone please tell me what's going on? First this crazy Kanaka drags me out of bed without even kissing me, and now we find everyone out on deck and all excited!"

Captain Gringo said, "It looks like another attempt to blow Your Highness higher than a kite. Fortunately, Gaston smelled something burning just in time. Our prime suspect is your Chinese cook. So let's talk about him."

Manukai gasped and said, "Hung Chang? I can't believe it, Dick. He makes such great egg rolls!"

Gaston cut in, "I am sure he was a most ingenious and surprising chef, mon cher. The question is, who *else* could he have been working for, hein?"

Manukai turned to her skipper and said something in their own lingo. Kuruhai banged the palm of his hand against his brow and said, "Oh shit, that's right! He used to work for the German missionary on Konakona! But I thought you just said you didn't think it was the Germans who were playing so rough!"

Captain Gringo shrugged and asked, "What can I tell you? Sometimes a guy just guesses wrong, right?"

•   •   •

They kept the basement of the Puntarenas morgue as cool as possible. But, without true air conditioning, the atmosphere still left a lot to be desired. The naval attaché from the German consulate held a kerchief to his face as the morgue attendant switched on the overhead lights. But Von Linderhoff and the Costa Rican police captain were made of sterner stuff, or just knew better than to try.

The bodies of the German agents that Captain Gringo had left in the alley behind the whorehouse had been mistreated further before the police had finally found them in another alley a good three blocks away. They were missing their shoes and other valuables, and being rained on as they sprawled in the muddy yard of an abandoned house hadn't done wonders for their appearance, either. They lay side by side on marble slabs, their muddy flesh cold and pale where it showed.

The police officer said, "Their passports were missing, of course. But fortunately one of my men recalled seeing the two of them going in and out of your consulate a lot, and of course, we have few blue-eyed blonds in this part of the world. Can you gentlemen identify either of them for us?"

Von Linderhoff said, "Of course. This one's Herr Dorfler and the other's name is Vogel. As you correctly assumed, they worked for my trade mission at the consulate. They were, ah, file clerks. Where did your men find them?"

"Not where they were killed, Señor. They were already a bit stiff when someone rolled them over a garden wall to be found in due course in rather grotesque positions. The one you call Vogel had been stabbed in the back, by an expert. The other had been *shot* in the back. There are no powder stains on his clothing, so that was the work of an expert as well. We were hoping you could give us some indication as to motive. It is odd to find two minor employees of your consulate murdered and robbed on the same day, do you not agree?''

Von Linderhoff shrugged and replied, ''You would know better than us how safe the streets you patrol might be, Captain. I can think of no motive other than robbery. They were, as you say, minor employees, not involved in any important matters.''

The Costa Rican looked politely at the naval attaché, who removed the kerchief from his face long enough to say, ''I did not even know them. I may have seen them about the consulate, but they did not work for my section.'' Then he covered his face again. It didn't really help.

Von Linderhoff said, ''Naturally, as soon as your own coroner releases the bodies to us, we shall ship them back to the Fatherland for proper burial. Meanwhile, is it possible to have them, ah, embalmed?''

The Costa Rican cop nodded with an agreeable smile and said, ''Most of what you are smelling is a woman fished out of the harbor yesterday. If someone doesn't claim her soon, we may have to put her back. Rock salt, as you may have noticed, has its limitations.''

He nodded to the attendant and they all left. Outside, Von Linderhoff waited until the Costa Rican officer had shaken hands with them and gone the other way before he told the naval attaché, ''*I* can play rough, too. I have been trying to handle the matter in a civilized way. But when one is dealing with mad dogs, one does not simply wave the gun about. One *shoots!* Is it safe to assume that gunboat of yours has something more serious than blank saluting rounds for its weaponry, Bachmann?''

The navy man looked uncomfortable and replied, ''We are of course ready for Der Tag any time the treacherous

British mean to start it. But we are hardly authorized to lob one-fifty-fives at anyone without a declaration of war!"

"What do call what just happened to Dorfler and Vogel, a declaration of *love*?"

"No, but they were professional secret agents paid to accept certain risks, even in peacetime, Herr Von Linderhoff! What you are asking of the Kriegsmarine is another matter entire! The gunboat Seeshlange is hardly a spy vessel! She openly and proudly flies the flag of the Fatherland, and have you forgotten the Monroe Doctrine? The Yankees would have a fit if we openly fired on anything in these waters!"

Von Linderhoff's voice dropped a few degrees, from already cool to icy, as he said flatly, "I am not *asking* the Seeshlange to do anything. I am *ordering* it. Have you forgotten who is the senior official of the Reich here, Bachmann?"

The uniformed officer answered just as coldly. "I am well aware of our respective ranks, Herr Linderhoff. But I still take my orders from the Kriegsmarine, not Military Intelligence! My orders are to cooperate with you, not to get Germany into a war Der Kaiser may not have been planning to have this season! I shall have to cable Berlin for authorization before we shoot even your mad dogs with one-fifty-fives, in American waters!"

Von Linderhoff grimaced and said, "Do you know what I think is going to happen when Der Tag arrives? I think everyone is going to be waiting for permission to fire as the enemy marches up the Unter Den Linden! This is an *emergency*, you blockheaded Bavarian!"

"Nevertheless, I must have authorization from Berlin before I order Seeshlange and her people into warlike action."

"Then let's *do* so, damn it! How long will it take you to cable home and get your damned authorization?"

Bachmann shrugged and said, "Less than twenty-four hours if the Admiral is not at his country estate. Perhaps sooner if he agrees. Personally, I still think you are out to crush a cockroach with a steamroller. Have you ever seen what a one-fifty-five does to everything all around when it hits?"

"I have. Blowing the bastards to bloody hash is less than they deserve!"

By the time the sun had flashed green and vanished, everyone aboard the Orotiki but Kuruhai had calmed down a bit. The big skipper still wanted to weigh anchor and charge the blackbirder base like a bull under sail. But as he kept drinking to soothe his nerves, he was too pooped to swat a fly by the time the extra weapons were smuggled aboard, so nobody was paying any attention to him.

The soldiers of fortune took the tarp-wrapped machine guns to Manukai's spacious quarters, by royal command; and as they unwrapped them on the rug while the princess watched—interested but ignorant of such matters—Captain Gringo said, "Okay, this Maxim could use more oil, but it's not in bad shape. How do you like your Browning, Gaston?"

Gaston growled, "I can man a machine gun in a pinch, but this species of junk seems to have been used as an agricultural implement more recently."

He unscrewed the side plate, disengaged the action, and added, "I take that back. It's been soaking in a cesspool for some time. But at least there is so much oily shit ground into the parts they have not rusted too badly. Give me time to completely strip and reassemble this abused child, and she just might fire again someday."

Captain Gringo adjusted the head spacing on his own weapon as he told Gaston, "You'll have plenty of time. I'm leaving you here as I scout the Guardian Bank with those fishermen, if they ever get here. I don't think anyone will feel up to rushing this schooner while I'm gone; but if they do, you, the crew's rifles, and that Browning ought to discourage hell out of them."

If he'd expected an argument from the pragmatic little Frenchman, he didn't get one. Gaston nodded and said, "Oui, I could hold that gangplank against all comers *without* a machine gun. But I'd better fix this one and haul the gangplank in just the same, hein?"

Captain Gringo consulted his watch and began to rewrap the Maxim as he said, "Let it go for now. We'd better get this one and its ammo amidships in case that fishing lugger ever shows up."

He glanced up at the big Kanaka girl and asked, "Is it okay for Gaston to leave this junk here and clean it later, Honey?"

She smiled fondly at both of them and replied, "Gaston sure isn't about to spend the night in anyone *else's* quarters, Dick. By the way, don't you mean to say aloha properly before you sail out of my life for Tangaroa-knows-how-long?"

He laughed and said, "We'll have a celebration when I get back. I may need my strength out on those reefs."

"Hell, Dick, you got a machine gun; and how much running around do you expect to be doing on a bitty boat. Let's have a nukilua *now*!"

Captain Gringo hefted the wrapped machine gun to his shoulder, got to his feet, and said, "I'll send Gaston right back to you. But first he has to help me get underway."

She didn't argue. But she was getting undressed as the two of them left. Outside, Gaston sighed and said, "You might have at least made la zigzig with her *once,* you lazy child. I'm getting too old to keep oversized sex maniacs contented.''

"You'll just have to try harder. I don't want Kuruhai jumping the gun while I'm not around to stop him, and she's the only person on board with the rank to stop the skipper without busting his head.''

"I know. Mon dieu, the things my tongue and I have to go through just to stay alive!''

"Does she really like that as much as fucking?''

"Merde alors, if there is anything of a sexual nature that big spoiled brat doesn't like, I've yet to find it; and I have already explored her body to the point of fatigue! It's simply not just, Dick. Here you are leaving me alone with a shipload of nubile vahines, and all my talents are required for political fornication!''

He was still bitching about it as they placed the Maxim and its ammo cases against the starboard bulwark, amidships. They gazed over the side. It was a lot like staring into an inkwell. Farther out on the dark waters of the harbor, they could see the illuminated bridge and portholes of the German gunboat. But her outlines were invisible against the black velvet sky. Captain Gringo said, "If your recruits get here before moonrise, we'll have nothing to worry about. What time are we talking about?''

"Do I look like an almanac? The moon rose after midnight last night, and it's twenty minutes later every night, non?''

"Yeah, we still have plenty of time. But I still wish they'd get here so I could go round up those frauleins.''

"You mean to take both, Dick?''

"Have to. Only one of them speaks English, and we can't leave the sister who speaks only German stranded in a Spanish-speaking port. I might be able to talk the redhead into staying here with you and the others. But I still have to go *get* both. So where the hell is that fishing lugger?''

Gaston suggested, ''Why don't you get them now? By the time you get back, our fishing friends will have either arrived or we'll know they have had second thoughts. In either case, those German girls will be as safe here as anyone could be at Mamma Rosa's, non?''

Captain Gringo said, ''Good thinking. It shouldn't take me more than half an hour.''

As he crossed the deck to the gangway, little Atanua intercepted him to ask if he wanted to make more nukinuki with her now that things were calming down aboard the schooner. He laughed and said, ''Another time. But you could do me another favor, Honey. I need someone from your crew who speaks both English and your own lingo, in case I need a translator.''

Atanua said, ''You gottem, Sweet Haole. Me talkee good as me fuckem.''

''I doubt that very much. I had a Kanaka *boy* in mind, Atanua.''

She giggled and asked, ''You likee *boy* better than *vahine*, you naughty-naughty? Me talkee Haole more better than any boy aboard except skipper, and I no think Kuruhai takem in he ass!''

Captain Gringo couldn't tell if she was fibbing. There wasn't time to argue about it. He nodded and said, ''Okay, stick around. I have to get a couple of other vahines we'll be bringing along. This sure is shaping up to be a silly combat patrol.''

''You wanna makem nukinuki along three vahines at once, big crazy cock?''

He laughed again, patted her bare brown hide fondly, and said, ''Sure. A crowded stinky fishing boat is just the place to stage an orgy.'' Then he was on his way before she could ask how come. Atanua might or might not come in handy if they got a chance to talk to any of the captives. But a sense of humor didn't seem to be her strong point.

He made it to Mamma Rosa's through the dark side streets of Puntarenas without getting in any trouble. Because he wanted to keep it that way, he circled to enter via the back door of the posada. The door was locked but not barred, so he picked the lock with the leather punchblade of his all-purpose pocketknife. As he moved quietly toward the front along the dark corridor, he was glad he hadn't knocked. He heard guttural voices muttering from somewhere up front. He didn't understand enough German to matter, but he knew few of the working-class guests of Mamma Rosa spoke it conversationally!

Drawing his .38, the big Yank eased his way to the front vestibule. It was blacked out. But a sliver of lamplight striped the tile floor, coming from the front door to Mamma Rosa's quarters. The landlady's door was barely ajar. The object peeking out of the slit to cover the front entrance didn't look like a cuckoo. It looked more like the muzzle of a twelve-gauge.

The shotgun was covering the front door with Captain Gringo's unexpected angle of approach blind to the idiot holding it. So Captain Gringo eased silently over to the same wall and then oozed like lava toward the ambush on the balls of his softly booted feet. Inside, someone was muttering in German again; and the guy nearer the door, with the scatter-gun, apparently was telling him to calm down and shut up. That made sense. Should anyone they didn't want to murder open the front door, they just had to lie doggo in Mamma Rosa's room until the guest went on upstairs. They were old pros, even if one of them seemed a little nervous this evening.

Captain Gringo eased to the angle the crude wrought-iron hinges made with the rough stucco he was sliding along. The larger slit that the guy with the gun was peering out wasn't the only one, thanks to the way the door was hung. Captain Gringo's wary eye was invisible to those inside as he peeked over the top of a hinge strap.

He liked what he saw. Mamma Rosa lay on the floor in a far corner, bound and gagged. A white-clad thug across the room had his back to everyone as he peered out at the street approach through a slit in the wooden shutters. The one training the twelve-gauge on the inside of the front entrance was, of course, almost smack against the door. So Captain Gringo couldn't see much of him. But he didn't have to. He knew he'd just have to move fast as hell.

He did. He grabbed the latch with his left hand, planted the toe of his right boot against the bottom of the door so it could neither open nor shut without his permission, and simply fired three rounds through the planking for openers!

The gunman inside howled in anguish as hot lead and oak splinters tore through his startled flesh. By then Captain Gringo had hauled the door open and grabbed the barrel of the twelve-gauge out of thin air as the first victim fell.

It turned out to be a wise move. Like most men who carried six-shooters through a life filled with surprises, Captain Gringo always packed his with one empty chamber under the hammer. So he only had two rounds left for the bozo by the window, and while he nailed him nicely twice as he whirled from the shutters, gun in hand, neither round hit anything vital and the guy was tough enough to raise his own weapon—albeit too confused, or hurt, to hit Captain Gringo with his first wild shot.

He didn't get to fire again. Twirling the captured shotgun like a drum major, Captain Gringo fired it like a pistol, lefthanded, to blow the already shot-up sneak's head half off with a blast of number-nine buck!

Then he moved all the way in, slammed the door after him, and dropped the scatter-gun between the sprawled bodies to kneel and get to work on Mamma Rosa's gag and bonds, with his empty .38 on the tiles between them.

He removed her gag first. She gasped, "Oh Ricardo, I was so afraid they would kill you and then kill me before they left!"

He said, "I noticed. Nothing happened here just now, should anyone ask. Got that?"

"Si, I run a most respectable posada. The shots I just heard must have come from some rougher part of the neighborhood."

He chuckled and went to work on her wrists. The sons of bitches had tied them with a knot he wasn't familiar with. So he was still working on it when a voice from outside called through the shutters, "Hey Rosa, it's me, Patrolman Vegas. Are you all right?"

From the floor, the landlady called back, "Si, but I am not dressed. What is going on out there? I was just awakened by the sound of gunplay, I think."

The cop called back, "Go back to sleep. Let La Policia worry about such matters, Rosa!"

As he tore off down the calle, tweeting his whistle for help or just to make noise, Captain Gringo got her wrists free and went to work on her ankles, saying, "I'm sure glad you know how to stay so respectable. Are those two German girls I brought here earlier still upstairs, Mamma Rosa?"

"Where else would they be? I do not think these ladrones were after any of my other guests. I don't think they even knew those girls were here. *I* certainly never told them! They said but a few words to me in Spanish as they bound and gagged me just now. But though I understood nothing of their barbarian language, I do not think 'Gringo' can mean anything but *you*, in German, no?"

"I doubt they were laying for Santa Claus. I'll worry later about how they figured I was on my way here. Do you really need help getting rid of their cadavers? I'm really in a hell of a hurry, Mamma Rosa!''

"Go with God, then, Ricardo mio. I know some enterprising youths who will help me clean up for their expensive shoes alone. What may be in their pockets is of course mine, for the *rent* they owe me, no?''

He laughed, but patted both stiffs down for ID anyway, explaining she was welcome to their goodies but that he'd still like to know who the hell they might have been. He found neither one had been thoughtful to carry his passport to work with him that evening. He grunted and told Mamma Rosa, "They're all yours. I might have seen this one bozo in the railroad depot up at San Jose. It's kind of hard to tell what he looked like, now.''

Mamma Rosa said something about getting a mop as he helped her to her feet. He didn't hang around to watch. He ducked out and headed upstairs, loading his .38 as he did so.

Hilda opened up on his third knock, her big blue eyes wider than the door as she asked, "Ach, Dick, what has been downstairs going on? We just heard what like a war sounded, und so frightened we are!''

He stepped in, shut the door after him, and saw they were both in the same mumus. Alfrieda was on the bed across the room, looking even more upset. He soothed them. "Nobody seems to have been after you. But tell me something: Did you come straight here from the schooner? No side trips to your hotel to pick something up?''

Hilda sighed and said, "We would have if we had known what kind of soap down the hall they had. But, nein, straight here we came like you told us to. Und now, will you please tell us what ist going on, Dick?''

"On the way back to the schooner. On the double. The back way ought to still be safe.''

The blonde didn't argue, but her redheaded sister who

didn't speak English kept asking dumb questions in German along the way until Captain Gringo told Hilda to tell her to shut up, adding, "People in this neck of the woods notice unusual voices, thank god."

So they were moving silently as he smuggled them across the dimly lit quay and back aboard the Orotiki. He sat them on a hatch cover and told them to keep up the good work while he checked with Gaston.

For once, things seemed to be going right. Gaston introduced him to a husky Costa Rican called Alberto, who said last names were not important between men of the world and added that the Maxim was already aboard a vessel they could call 'La Paloma' for this trip.

Captain Gringo moved to the starboard rail to stare down over the side before he said, "Bueno." The two-masted lugger was a lot smaller than the schooner, of course, but larger than he'd expected. She was decked from mainmast forward, with a fair-size cabin amidships and the forepeak clear save for a small chain-locker hatch. He asked Alberto how fast the rather beamy boat could sail down the trades, and her skipper said, "Five, maybe six knots. Beating our way back, against the winds, will of course take us longer. But, on the other hand, La Paloma sails faster with the winds abeam, if we are talking about outrunning anyone."

Gaston started to mutter something about steam-driven gunboats. But Captain Gringo kicked his shin and told Alberto, "We'd better get started, then. Has my friend here issued you your front money and new rifles?"

"Si, that gives us eight armed men aboard, aside from you and me, Captain Gringo. Nine Krags and a machine gun ought to keep the sharks at bay, no?"

"That's all the men you have, Skipper?"

"That's all the *room* we have. Naturally, men planning to be away from home at least forty-eight hours, maybe even longer, could hardly be expected to leave their mujeres behind."

"Jesus, we've got eight *women* on board, aside from the three I have to bring with me?"

"No, Captain Gringo. We have *nine* Costa Rican girls aboard. Do I look like a man who plays with himself?"

Captain Gringo knew better than to argue. Like other sane men, regular Hispanic merchant seamen of course had to sail stag. But guys used to putting out to sea for only a day's fishing at a time naturally expected to get laid every night. He turned to Gaston and said, "Okay, we'd better break out nine more rifles, just in case."

Gaston grinned and said, "I already have, knowing how you feel about unarmed baggage just being in the way in a firefight. What about the Kanaka translator and the two frauleins?"

"Negative. All three are sort of feminine above and beyond the call of duty, and I mean to keep them below decks if there's any trouble."

"Unless, of course, you get sunk?"

"What can I tell you? How far could any dame swim with an eight-pound rifle? Let's get the show on the road, Alberto. At five or six knots we're timing it about right if we shove off right now."

The Costa Rican swung over the side to drop into La Paloma and take command as Captain Gringo gathered the mumu-clad German girls and the nearly naked Atanua. As he helped them down into the lugger, Hilda asked how long they'd be on the sort of stinky thing, and he said, "About eighteen to twenty hours, getting out there. Don't ask when we'll be coming back."

"Such long to sail, Dick? Ist only a hundred nautical miles about, nicht wahr?"

"Yeah, well, the yacht you hired may have made better than five knots. But add it up and you'll see it takes twenty hours to sail a hundred at five. Look on the bright side. We'll be sighting the Guardian Bank's rocks and reefs just after sunset tomorrow night. That sure beats sailing in by broad-ass *daylight,* until we have an educated guess about what's *out* there!''

By the time La Paloma stood well out to sea, apparently having left Puntarenas unobserved, Captain Gringo and Alberto had organized at least a little order out of the general chaos aboard the crowded little lugger.

The skipper's own stuff, a pretty but hard-looking mestiza called Beatriz, manned the helm as Gringo and Alberto crouched in the bow. Captain Gringo asked what was in the chain locker under them, and Alberto said, ''Nada. Is empty. As you see, La Paloma rides easier with her bows light, and we usually tie her up each night in any case. So for why should we carry anchor chains? And for why should this be of importance to you, Captain Gringo?''

The American rapped the solid decking with his knuckles before he replied, ''I may have to drive some nails in your deck here. Permiso?''

''Si, if you have a good reason.''

''I have. It's tedious as hell to have one's machine-gun tripod washed overboard by an unexpected swell. I want to mount the Maxim here on the peak. If I have to cover our stern unexpectedly, I can always fire free-hand over the transom. But the unused chain locker makes a handy machine-gun nest up here where there's no other cover for me.''

Alberto opened the small hatch and folded it back against the cabin bulkhead, saying, ''Help yourself. You will find hammer and nails in the ship's carpenter chest under my chart table when you need them. I am the ship's carpenter as well as skipper. So you do not have to explain to anyone.''

Captain Gringo nodded, let himself down into the chain locker, and struck a match. It was clean, at least, and the triangular space, while small, was large enough for what he had in mind. He climbed back out and told Alberto, ''If I could have some matting and bedding, the three mujeres with me might be more out of the way up here.''

The Costa Rican grinned and said, ''We have heard you are quite a man, Captain Gringo, but ... all *three* of them?''

Captain Gringo laughed at the ridiculous picture and said, ''As a matter of fact, I may need a chaperone or more for at least one of them. Actually, I want them all in one place where I can keep an eye on them if things get exciting. None of them speak Spanish, and we already have a large-enough female crowd aboard for more milling around than I like to think about, if things get *too* exciting!''

Alberto looked a little worried as he said, ''Most of our mujeres have been out to sea before. The Frenchman assured us we would only be called on for to snoop about out there, not for to engage in a sea battle. One hopes he was not selling us the brick of gold?''

Captain Gringo tried to sound surer than he really felt. ''The deal you made still stands, Alberto. All we have to do is pinpoint the exact islet those kidnapped pearl divers are being held on. Once we do, we've got a bigger vessel and a bigger gang to hit them with. Do I look like the kind of idiot who'd attack an armed camp with a handful of fisherfolk?''

Alberto sighed and said, ''I don't know. My Beatriz said she served as an adelita under you one time, and that you were a most aggressive guerrilla leader!''

Captain Gringo frowned thoughtfully at Alberto in the

darkness as he tried to picture the tough little mutt at the helm again. He didn't recall ever laying her, and she was pretty enough to remember. But one heart-shaped brown mestiza face looked much like any other amid a gaggle of camp followers. He asked cautiously, "Where did she say all this was going on?"

Alberto said, "A few months ago, down along the border. The soldado whose adelita she was at the time was killed in that fight you had with the Colombians. Beatriz said she did not think you would remember her even though, she says, you were very kind to all your people."

Captain Gringo shrugged and said, "It's a small world. I remember the battle. I guess you don't want me remembering your woman any better, eh?"

The skipper chuckled and said, "Es verdad. She says you screwed hell out of half the adelitas in camp down that way."

"Oh, she's just telling war stories. I never touched anything like *half* the girls in that guerrilla crew. I was leading a goddam *battalion*!"

The dirty conversation had restored Alberto's humor by the time they made it aft. The skipper twitted his girl at the helm about her famous Captain Gringo not remembering her; and from the way she scowled by the light of the rising moon, she didn't enjoy being teased. So Captain Gringo nodded at her and said, "Buen'noches, Beatriz, I *thought* I recognized you from the old outfit, but that fisherman's sweater threw me off."

The pretty little mestiza stuck her tongue out at Alberto and said, "You see?" So the skipper laughed easily and replied, "In god's truth, Querida, you are not as easy to recognize when your tits don't show."

Inside the overcrowded cabin, the mood was less jolly. The German redhead, Alfrieda, was seasick; and while she didn't understand the growling Spanish around her, it was obvious someone was going to do something just awful if she threw up in there.

Captain Gringo told Hilda to get her outside as he, in turn, wedged himself through the crowd to get the machine gun, along with its tripod and ammo.

A fisherman cursed him as he had to move his butt off an ammo case. Little Atanua, wedged in a corner, asked if there was anything she could do to help. He told her to get the carpenter's chest and follow him. She did, as he climbed over people getting back out.

When he did, Alfrieda was puking over the stern as, at the helm, Beatriz suggested sweetly that when she tasted hair she should swallow, lest she puke her own asshole. Fortunately, the German girl didn't understand, so she didn't have the rough seagirl's humor to cope with. She had enough to worry about, even with her sister comforting her.

He left them to that problem as, once Atanua joined him, he led her forward. They dropped their load in the peak, and he told her to hang on to everything as the lugger took another sea swell under her buff stern and threatened to bury her bows in green water. She said, "Yes, my word, these people don't know shit about makem friends with Kai."

He started nailing the pads of the tripod to the deck as he asked her who the hell this 'Kai' was, adding they already had too many people aboard.

She laughed and said, "Oh, silly big cock, 'Kai' is what my people are calling the sea. These alleesame crazy Costa Ricans don't savvy you gottem make friends with Kai and Raki—that's the sky—before you sailem out of sight of Papa, she's the land. Why you not put out with *Kanaka* crew, you big silly cock?"

"The Costa Rican crew comes with the Costa Rican

fishing boat, of course. And do you have to keep calling me a silly cock, you silly cunt?''

She laughed and said, "Oh goody, let's put silly cock in silly cunt! We alleesame alone up here and no place else on board for makee nukinuki! My word, how you 'spose them others gonna makem nukinuki in such crowdee cabin? S'pose they puttem out lightee for nukinuki, somebody bound to wind up in wrong hole.''

She laughed again and added, "Maybe that more fun, my word. But they all stinkee from wear too much clothes in hot stinkee cabin. So me just wanna make nukinuki along you!''

He told her to behave as he mounted the Maxim on the tripod, drove a square of nailheads to brace an ammo box, and opened it to feed the canvas-web ammo belt into the action. He armed the gun and put it on safety, warning her, "Don't you touch this, ever."

She said, "Pooh, no wanna makee gun shoot. Wanna make *you* shoot, in *me*!''

It was just as well he didn't take her up on the offer. For Beatriz came forward, carrying a pile of bedding. As she flopped down next to the Kanaka girl with it, she said, "Alberto's at the helm now. He'll be there for four hours. Do you really remember me from the old outfit, Captain Gringo?''

He assured her he did, even though he didn't; and of course did so in Spanish. So Atanua pouted and asked in English, "Hey, wassamatter this Haole cunt? *She* wanna make nukinuki, too?''

Captain Gringo told her to shut up, opened the hatch, and added she should go below and line the nest with the bedding. So she laughed and proceeded to do so, making lewd suggestions about the possibilities of such a cozy love nest as he in turn explained to the ex-adelita that she was slightly nuts.

The mestiza sighed and said, "I don't suppose there'd be room for *five* down in that chain locker, would there?"

He frowned thoughtfully and kept his voice desperately devoid of anything that could be taken the wrong way as he replied, "I don't see how the four of us are going to fit and, ah, you have your own hombre to, ah, keep company with, no?"

She shrugged and said, "If you say so. When a woman has no man, she must take what she can get. Will you tell me something, truthfully? I promise I will not get angry, Captain Gringo."

"What is it you want to know, Beatriz?"

"Down south, that time, when the soldado who owned me got shot on the last day of the fighting . . ."

"We lost a lot of good men that time, before we won."

"Si, and the adelita of one of the first we lost on that campaign wound up in your tent. But when *I* was left alone . . ."

He shook his head wearily and said, "A lot of you girls might have wound up feeling a little left out, Beatriz. But, hell, how many adelitas can fit in one sleeping bag? I led you all down there to fight, not to . . . you know."

"I know. You led us well. And when it was over you saw we all got paid. You did not treat us with the ingratitude of some leaders. That is for why I am no longer interested in the military life. You are trying for to be gallant. I know you do not remember me. But I remember how *kind* you were when you told me my soldado had bought it. I remember you gave me his back pay before we disbanded, too. But, si, a woman can feel left out just the same. I still think I was prettier than some of the adelitas you took a more personal interest in."

He patted her shoulder and said, "You were. I do remember you. But as you say, your soldado was killed at the end, and what kind of a man would trifle with a woman still in mourning? You probably remember I left suddenly, when I was recalled to headquarters. That's why I may not have said adios as you may have wished.''

She smiled wistfully in the moonlight and murmured, ''Ay que linda you lie! I remember all too well the fancy blanca you left with in that private coach. I wished for to scratch her eyes out! But you are right, the dead past is gone forever and tomorrow is so often too late. I shall not make a pest of myself, Captain Gringo. For one thing, Alberto hits when he is angry. I shall not even scratch any eyes out, if only you will do me one favor for old time's sake.''

So he rose and helped her to her feet, staring aft over her to make sure the sails were blocking the view from the helm as he said softly, ''I suppose an old army buddy deserves a favor, Soldada. So name it.''

She reached up to draw his face down to hers as they kissed in the moonlight. Then she sobbed and said, ''I thought that would do it. I should have known better. But do not worry, I know when I am not wanted.''

He wasn't so sure about that as she made her way aft, leaving him with a tingle in his pants he hadn't noticed before. She sure kissed good and, Jesus, to think he'd passed that up when it had been all his, if only he'd known at the time!

He grimaced and moved aft himself to gather in the rest of his flock. When he reached the stern, Beatriz was nowhere to be seen. At the helm, her new man, Alberto, said, ''I think this redhead could be cured by an hour's rest under a banana tree. But we don't grow them this far out to sea. Did my mujer fix you up all right, Captain Gringo?''

''As well as she could under the circumstances. Thanks for the bedding.''

''Por nada. But could you get these two out of here? I

am a formidable sailor, but the swells are getting rougher out here and there is a limit to how much puke even I wish for to inhale with the vessel rolling so.''

Captain Gringo took Alfrieda by her free arm and said, ''We'd best bed her down, Hilda. Atanua should have her corner of the chain locker ready by now.''

''Mein Gott! In der *bow* you want her to try und rest when in der *stern* she is upgethrowing all she's eaten since Bremerhaven we left?''

''The ground swells are actually lifting the stern worse than the bows on this tack, Hilda. By the way, Alberto, wouldn't she ride steadier if you took the swells on the stern quarter?''

The skipper nodded, but said, ''She'd ride even sweeter if we tacked across the trades north or south. But I assumed you wished for to sail to the Guardian Bank, dead ahead and directly downwind, no?''

''I hope so. Forget it. Sometimes us landlubbers ask stupid questions. You know where to find me if you need me.''

He led the two German girls forward, clinging to the cabin coaming rail with his free hand as La Paloma kept trying to slither out from under them. He called out to Atanua, who reached up to help them get the redhead below. The girl warned, ''My word, if she throws up down here, me gonna shit in her face!''

Captain Gringo struck a match for light as Hilda tried to make her seasick sister comfortable. It was impossible, of course, but once the mumu-clad redhead had her head down in the padded wedge of the bow, she at least stopped moaning so loudly. He told Hilda to tell her to draw her legs up, for Chrissake; but even with Alfrieda in a sick-baby ball, there still wasn't room for the rest of them to lie down much, let alone stretch out. He told the girls to make themselves comfortable as he stood with his shoulders out the little hatchway, finding that, as planned, he could swing the Maxim nicely on its tripod from this position.

There wasn't a thing to aim at, of course. Not even the cold green whitecaps one often saw at night in tropic waters. The little critters that lit the foam up at night down here had apparently dropped deeper into less roiled water. That was something to study on. The seagoing lightning bugs might know something he or even the skipper didn't! He'd noticed how critters always seemed to sense a storm before humans. But, on the other hand, the prevailing trade winds tended to shift south or even reverse before the Carib god Hurikan showed up. So what the hell.

He'd just told himself how nice and reassuring the trades were blowing that night when they blew an unusual amount of sea under La Paloma's stern and the bows went under.

Not far. Not even enough to matter, had not the hatch he was standing in been open. But enough green water slopped over the unrailed bows to make him sincerely happy the gun tripod and ammo box were secured by nails when the sheet of brine swept through them, smacked into the coaming of the hatch, and soaked him from the shirtfront up.

He growled, "Thanks. I needed that," as below him in the darkness, Hilda wailed, "Zum Teufel! Are we sinking already?"

He called down, "Not yet. What are *you* bitching about? I caught most of it, and I think that was it for now."

"Easy for you to say, Dick! I am to the skin soaked!"

Atanua laughed at her in the dark and said, "It's what you pink people get for dressing silly. Me just gotta take off little tapa, wipe me off, and good as new. Takem off mumu before you get chilled, dumb Haole Hilda."

Hilda was doing no such thing, judging from the way she was cursing in German. Captain Gringo couldn't see what was going on down there in the dark, but apparently Hilda found it unsettling, because she switched back to English, sort of, to gasp, "Ach, crazy savage! Wass are you *doing*?"

Captain Gringo wondered too, as he felt familiar hands getting familiar indeed with him, down there. As Atanua began to unbuckle his belt, he called down, "Cut that out, you little nut! I don't *want* my pants off, damn it!"

But she insisted, "Sure you do. You all wet. You wanna die of bloody-lung fever and never make nukinuki again, dumb prick?"

He started to drop below and make her behave. But just then he spotted a flicker of light off to their south and snapped, "Cut it out, no shit! I think I just saw another vessel in the distance, and this is no time to be caught with one's pants down literally!"

But Atanua didn't listen well as Captain Gringo called back, "Hey, Alberto, ten points off the port bow?"

The Costa Rican called back, "I saw it. If I see it again, I'm tacking to starboard. I don't see it now, and it might have been moonlight on a whitecap."

So La Paloma sailed steadily on through the night as, in the deeper darkness below, Atanua pulled Captain Gringo's pants down and proceeded to suck him off while another lady swore in German and kept asking in English if they were both mad.

He sighed and called down, "I told you she was nuts. Don't look if it bothers you. I'm starting to *like* it, I'm ashamed to say, and, well, we have been sort of friendly before."

"Mein Gott! You are both savages, und also a crime against nature committing! I won't have it!"

He closed his eyes and hissed as the less inhibited island girl who was *actually* having it started sucking harder, with considerable skill. He knew he shouldn't; but what the hell, how shocked could anyone else get if a guy came right?

He was coming for sure, one way or the other. So he dropped down inside to lay Atanua old-fashioned while— braced in a semi-seated position against the hull—Hilda covered her face with her hands and gasped, "Please, one of you your foot in mein lap has; und if you don't mind, I do not wish to be involved in your disgusting orgy!"

It wasn't him. So Captain Gringo said, "Atanua, get your foot out of the lady's crotch," as he moved in hers with enthusiasm, despite his embarrassment. For Atanua screwed even better than she sucked.

She wrapped her brown legs around his naked butt, asking if that was better, while Hilda gasped, "I wish you two would behave!"

Wedged in the bow with her feet almost touching them, Alfrieda asked, sickly, what was going on. Hilda must have put it pungently, in German, because the redhead sat up with renewed interest in life to giggle. "Ach, das ist so!" she said.

Captain Gringo was now too hot to care much about public opinion, so he just pounded away until he'd ejaculated in the little Kanaka's orgasmic flesh. As sanity began to return, of course, he felt sort of dumb with two pretty girls he'd never even kissed staring down at them accusingly.

He felt even dumber when La Paloma took more green water over the bow and gave them all another shower through the hatch. He dismounted from Atanua, stood up, and hauled in the Maxim and ammo, leaving the nailed-down tripod to take its chances on deck as he closed the hatch, plunging the chain locker into pitch darkness. As he found a corner to wedge the Maxim, Hilda said in a disgusted voice, "Ach, *now* you modest wish to act? Ist too late. We know all your secrets, you wicked jungen!"

He pulled off his wet shirt in the darkness, wadded it,

and tucked it out of the way with his holstered .38 atop it
as he sighed sheepishly and said, "You girls knew I was
sort of wild when you tried to hire me. I'm not taking any
money from either of you, by the way. So let's be a little
charitable about my uncouth manners, okay? I'm a guy. I
enjoy sex. I'm not bothering either of *you* for any, so cut
the maidenly bullshit."

Then, as he heard Atanua giggling somewhere in the
dark, he chuckled and added, "Speaking of maidenly
bullshit, I left a maiden somewhere around here just now."

He reached for Atanua's naked flesh in the confusing
darkness, and as the lugger rolled, wound up with someone's
silk-covered tit instead. He said, "Sorry, Hilda," and she
asked, "Sorry for what?" as her redheaded sister giggled
and said something in German that sounded pretty naughty.
So he left his hand where it was as the English-speaking
blonde gasped and said, "You animal! Leave mein poor
sister alone!"

But he moved closer, and Alfrieda didn't seem to mind
as he said, "Let the lady speak for herself, Hilda. It seems
to be just what she needed for her seasickness."

Hilda laughed in the dark despite herself, and as the
redhead took him in her arms, coyly, translated and asked
in German what the hell was going on. So Alfrieda told
her, in the same lingo, while Captain Gringo helped her
out of her wet mumu. The blonde gasped. "How dare you
treat mein poor sister so?" she said as Atanua, who could
only follow part of what was going on, bitched from
another corner of the padded triangular darkness, "Hey,
who he making nukinuki alongside *now*, damn crazy cock?"

Hilda sobbed, "Shut up, you cannibal!" as she rolled to
her knees, groping in the dark in an attempt at rescue. She
grabbed Captain Gringo's bounding wet rump, still chilled
by the bounding sea outside, and gasped in dismay.

Atanua asked her conversationally, "Whassamatter, they

making nukinuki?'' and Hilda answered, ''Worse! They seem to be *fucking,* und mein sister does not even English speak!''

Captain Gringo laughed as the redhead chewed his ear, and he said, ''I've noticed I make out better, quicker, with dames I don't get to bullshit with. I think sometimes us poor guys blow things worse by bullshitting a dame who's already halfway sold!''

''Do you have to talk dirty while you my poor sister treat dirty, you monster?'' Hilda asked with a sniff. But when she asked Alfrieda in German if he was hurting her, the redhead told her to shut up or, better yet, ask this nice young man to move a little faster.

Hilda did no such thing, of course. But the redheaded widow had her own methods of getting her message across as she bumped and ground under Captain Gringo. So he considered it his duty as a gentleman to respond in kind to a lady who obviously hadn't been getting any lately. They were going at it hot and heavy when the lugger rolled unexpectedly and everyone wound up in a wriggling pile against the starboard slope. Nobody but the blonde had anything on by this time, and even Hilda felt pretty sexy in that wet silk mumu. So Atanua pulled the bigger girl's mumu hem up around her chilled hips and said, ''Me cold on outside. Still hot on inside. If him busy alongside other vahine, you and me make feely-feely, okay?''

''Ach, nein! Do I look like a lesbian?'' protested Hilda, even as the free-thinking Atanua started fingering her, answering, ''Me no can see. So me no know what you lookem like. But s'pose you feely *me,* my word? You goddam poor sport? Whassamatter you no wanna help a sistah out? Don't you likee my feely-feely, silly cunt?''

Hilda moaned, ''Ach, hilfe! I think I am being by a finger raped!'' So Alfrieda asked in German what was going on and when Hilda told her, laughed lewdly and made an even lewder suggestion. She and Captain Gringo had in the meantime climaxed together, so he was in shape to ask Hilda what they were talking about. She gasped, "You are all insane! This crazy cannibal ist making lesbian advance, und now mein crazy sister is suggesting we trade partners und . . . Oooooh, Gott im Himmel, I *also* seem to be crazy going, because if we don't I am about to mitt another woman come!"

He said he was sure she didn't want anything like that to happen. The lugger heeled the other way, and he grabbed her on the roll. They somehow wound up wedged in the angle of the bow with him on top, as elsewhere in the dark the other two girls were giggling dirty as hell about whatever *they* were up to, or down on. Hilda protested, "Wait! What do you think you are to me doing! I am nicht that kind of girl und . . . Ach du lieber, I see I *am*, und can't we this wet silk get out of the way, mein Schatz?"

He thought it was a swell idea, and so, once they had her naked, too, Hilda forgot her own inhibitions, and while she might not have *started* with the saucy redhead's libido, she made up for lost time once the ice of her reserve had been broken. He noticed that her bigger breasts cushioned his chest just right while her slimmer hips were novel, too. So despite the demands already made on him in recent memory, Captain Gringo was able to keep it up and then some in the blonde's tighter and now inspired gates of paradise.

She naturally came ahead of him and, as he kept posting in the saddle at a comfortable lope, Hilda giggled and said, "This is nicht proper at alles! But at least it ist nicht *perverse*! What do you think those two bad girls are doing, Dick? Ist das what I think I hearing am? Ach, it sounds like two kitten licking cream, nicht wahr?"

He answered, "Don't ask unless you want to try it. I'm

game to trade partners again if you want to make a Roman night of it.''

"Don't be ridiculous! I am only fucking interested in, as well you know by now, you brute!''

But, of course, it was a long night, there was nothing else to do in there but catnap now and again—all jammed together and rubbing together as the bows rose and fell. So by morning everyone had done everything that didn't hurt to everyone else. Captain Gringo even got some sleep, since a mere male could only enjoy a limited number of orgasms, even entangled with three beautiful nymphomaniacs.

Fortunately he was awake when he heard footsteps on the deck above and rose just as the hatch popped open to shed some light on the subject. It was Beatriz. He didn't think she could see what was going on around his bare shins as she said, "I'm about to go on watch. But I just made Moors and Christians. Would you like for me to bring your breakfast trays forward or do you want to come aft? You must wish for to stretch your legs on deck by now, no?''

He told her they'd come aft and eat with the crew, mostly because he wanted to get rid of her poco tiempo. When he did, he ducked down and told the girls to get dressed, adding, "For god's sake, Hilda, that's your *sister* you're going sixty-nine with!''

Hilda sighed and said, "I know. We decided as long as we to hell were going for experimenting with unnatural lusts, we might as well incest also try.''

He hunkered down without further comment to haul on his pants at least, slapping Atanua's brown hand away from his weary balls. Then he mounted the machine gun on the tripod nailed to the deck again and told the three of them he'd bring them something else to eat in a while. Atanua giggled and said there was no hurry.

He climbed stiffly out and moved aft, where he found

Beatriz still dishing out the rice and beans in the cockpit.
One of the other Costa Ricans was at the helm. Beatriz
explained that her hombre, Alberto, was having breakfast
in bed. Captain Gringo wondered what else the skipper
had just had in bed, but it would have been unfair as well
as silly to ask. He'd noticed the main cabin was partitioned
into one large and a few smaller compartments. If it had
been his vessel and Beatriz had been his mujer, that's the
way he'd have worked it, too. He wondered, as he ate his
simple but hearty breakfast, why he was wondering about
things like that after an all-night orgy with three dames at
least as nice looking as old Beatriz. That was the trouble
with pretty women. No matter how many a guy had, he
always noticed one he couldn't have.

By now everyone else had been served. So he asked the
mestiza for what was left in the pot, in three tin dishes.
She served up breakfast for the girls, asking politely if the
redhead was still seasick. He told her Alfrieda had recovered
after a good night's rest and Beatriz looked away, blushing.
He didn't ask why. If she and Alberto shared the forward
compartment of the main cabin, they'd been sharing a thin
bulkhead between all concerned as well, and, yeah, Hilda
had been making a lot of noise.

He asked the Costa Rican girl, casually, if she spoke any
English. Her blush grew darker but her voice remained
calm as she answered, ''Si, a little. Let me help you with
the dishes for your, ah, good friends.''

He let her, since he didn't really have three hands. She
waited until they were out of earshot from anyone, amidships,
before she switched to not-bad English anyway and said,
''I should not speak behind Alberto's back. He is not a bad
man. But you and me are old comrades in arms, no?''

''What's been going on behind my back, the usual?''

''Si, the men have been discussing how far they mean to
follow you in this matter, Captain Gringo. They are

willing for to go out to the Guardian Bank, as they agreed. But you have the reputation for wildness, once you get to where you are going. Alberto says if you go crazy and start a fight out there, you are, how you say, on your own?"

He nodded soberly and said, "Thanks, old comrade. But don't worry your pretty little head about it. I'm not as crazy as some may think. The guns we brought along are just a precaution in case someone tries to start a fight with *us*. This is simply a scouting expedition. I'm not looking for a naval engagement with a bigger outfit."

"Do you really think my head is pretty, Captain Gringo?"

"The rest of you's not bad either, and you can call me 'Dick' if you want to."

She sighed and said, "Oh, I want to, muy mucho. But we never seem to meet when both of us are free. Forgive me, I mean no disrespect, but are you with all *three* of those other adelitas this time?"

He chuckled and said, "What can I tell you, there's always room for one more? I don't think we'd better take this any further, do you?"

"No, I fear I would wind up killing someone, and, of course, if Alberto found out he would probably wind up killing me."

The seas were rougher than usual for the time of the year, but the trades blew harder, so otherwise the sail went smoothly and at times La Paloma almost made six or even seven knots on the crests of the long ground swells. Captain Gringo spent most of the time lazing on deck as the rather monotonous day wore on. Around noon they spotted a smoke plume on the north horizon. But they never sighted the ship that was apparently steaming so importantly, and of course, if they couldn't make *her* out, she had no way of spotting a smaller vessel under sail alone to her south.

The three girls up forward had run out of naughty ideas, and came out on deck as well later in the day. Nobody but Captain Gringo seemed to notice the German girls had gotten their mumus mixed up. Atanua's tiny tapa cloth attracted more attention from the more severely brought-up crew. But there were things to be said for going to sea coed. So nobody bothered the nearly naked vahine.

In mid-afternoon, Captain Gringo went below to catch a little serious sleep, giving serious orders to the girls before he did so. Hence, though Atanua woke him up a few hours later by tugging on his dong, it was only to tell him the sun was setting again in case he wanted to do anything about it.

He went aft and ate tortillas and beans with the skipper and Beatriz, even though Atanua called him a sissy. Alberto said that at the rate they were sailing, they might make the outer reefs of the Guardian Bank just after sunset. Captain Gringo glanced up and said, "With that cloud cover, there should be some twilight until, say, eight-thirty. Can do?"

Alberto grimaced and replied, "It is in the tricky light just before dawn or after sunset that a sailor's eyes play tricks on him. I told you I do not know the waters ahead. I certainly hope those German sisters do. The tiny islands of the Guardian Bank are no place to be shipwrecked, even when they are not being held by piratical slavers, eh?"

Captain Gringo told him he worried too much and moved forward to make sure the Maxim was still there. It was. So was Hilda. The blonde was seated cross-legged with her back braced against the cabin. He asked where the redhead and Atanua were, and she said, "Below, acting silly again. Ich bin trying to break the habit. Now that I have mitt such vices experimented, I think I like men best.''

He sat beside her and said, ''I noticed, and I'm so glad. Now that we're, ah, sort of old friends, would you tell me a secret, Hilda?''

She shrugged and said, ''Ist no use trying to pretend mein sister und me virgins are, now. Perhaps in Bremerhaven Alfrieda und me a little wild were considered by the neighbors, growing up. But *you* also must have neighbors shocked in your own time, nicht wahr?''

He smiled thinly and said, ''That's not what I'm worried about right now. The charts say the islets ahead are all small and almost featureless. Alberto, back in the stern, has no idea where the hell we're making landfall. So let's talk about how you're going to be able to tell one patch of coral from another in lousy light.''

She shrugged and answered, ''It was your idea to use me as your pilot, Dick. I said I would know where we were if we were anywhere near the parts of the bank I have geseen. The last time we out here were, in a much faster yacht, we had to poke about among the deserted bits of land for the one mitt Halle und Feldmacher's compound on it gebuilt. Once we are anywhere near the island they occupy, it ist easy to see, over the horizon. Aside from tin roofing, they have also a watchtower in the middle of the slave camp gebuilt. It looks like ein water tower, except up in it they a machine gun like this one keep.''

''Are you sure it's a Maxim, not a Spandau?''

''Gott in Himmel, how should *I* know? I never up in the guard tower was. But while we were there they fired at some natives, powpowpow from up there. I think it was only to scare them. I don't know why.''

He grimaced and said, ''I do,'' as he took out a claro and lit it. Then he said, ''When a small band of guys are guarding a bigger bunch, they like to scare them a lot. Keeps prisoners from getting ideas about rushing their captors, and as you may have noticed, Kanakas are sort of impulsive. How many guards and how many prisoners are we talking about, by the way? Manukai could only tell me a mess of her people were being held out there, and that they had armed steam launches along with the tower gun you just cheered me up about. I'd feel better if I had some exact numbers, and you've been there.''

Hilda shook her head and said, "Exact numbers I can't give you, Dick. I told you they would not let us everything see. I remember the steam launches. At least two they have, mitt also machine guns mounted on the bows. The natives number maybe two hundred. Not all pearl divers are. Some work at other jobs for the blackbirders. Also some are house servants for the lazy company men. Some of the womens, now that I know Atanua, are no doubt there to provide *other* services for the blackbirders, nicht wahr?''

"Why jerk off when you don't have to? Okay, I can picture the overall layout. All I have to do now is pinpoint the exact island and the best way to approach it. Did you come in to lee or windward aboard that yacht?''

She thought and said, "Straight in, the way we are going, I think.''

"You think? You don't know? In these waters, most landings are made on the lee side of most islands, Honey.''

"Ach, ja, I remember our charter skipper mentioning this, now. He also said it was dangerous to have the harbor the prevailing winds facing. But on the lee side is all shoal water. That ist where the pearls are growing. Once der Guardian Bank must have one big flat island been. Now it ist slowly sen alles sinking, mitt only the bumps up gesticking.''

He nodded, said it made sense, and that all they could

do now was wait. So they did. It took a million years for the sun ahead of them to set. Then it took another million before the Costa Rican lookout called down that he saw breakers ahead in the purple twilight. So Captain Gringo yelled down into the chain locker for Atanua and the redhead to get dressed and move aft for Chrissake. Then, when they finally did so, he dropped down into the hatch with Hilda so they could stand side by side behind the machine gun as she conned them in, or tried to.

Alberto ordered the sails reefed halfway and swung broadside to the trades. They still moved La Paloma a-lee, albeit more slowly. Beatriz moved forward to tell Captain Gringo the skipper wanted to know what happened next. He told Hilda it was her turn. The German girl squinted west at what looked like seas breaking halfway up a big white mudpie and said, "I think it was more to the north we went. Ja, das rock in the middle of barren sand looks familiar. The main island was to the north, I am now sure."

Captain Gringo sent the Costa Rican girl aft with the message. La Paloma started moving north as Alberto ordered the lug sails higher, but she clawed off the leeward shoals with her helm hard over. A few minutes later Captain Gringo spied another island ahead and asked Hilda, "Well? I don't see any tin roofs, Doll."

She said, "Farther north. I am almost sure, now."

Then Beatriz returned to say they'd spotted a light *astern*, a bright one. So Captain Gringo climbed out to follow her aft, with the blonde trailing behind. In the cockpit, Alberto pointed at the chalky white skyglow to the south and said, "It's limelight. I have seen it before. Squid fishermen use it a lot for fishing at night."

Captain Gringo nodded and said, "So somebody must be fishing over that way, if not for squid, for something else. You say you coast fishermen seldom come out this far, Alberto?''

"Santa Maria, we *never* come out this far unless someone pays us to. For why would we wish to catch fish so far from land? How could we preserve them without ice, sailing upwind so far to the market, eh?"

"Makes sense. Let's swing back and take a peek at that mysterious limelight.''

Hilda protested, ''Dick, I am sure we did not so far *south* land.'' But he said, ''Yeah, and one boulder in the middle of a sand flat looks a lot like any other. Put about, Alberto. I've got another idea about limelights lit up just after dark. I heard they've been using them on Cuba, at those new concentration camps the Spanish have invented.''

Captain Gringo was right. As the blacked-out La Paloma moved south just outside the breaker line, a tall black tower surrounded by shinier metal roofing rose above the horizon, brightly illuminated by the chalk-white glare of limelight searchlights. Alberto, at the helm, said, ''Bueno. I can mark that island on the chart for you. So now we head back to the mainland, no?''

Captain Gringo said, ''Steady as she goes. I have to see where the captives are being held and if there's a fence to worry about or if they just use the sharks to keep everyone in at night.''

"You are going to get us all killed,'' muttered Alberto. But he kept his heading as others—some grumbling ominously about crazy gringo Peeping Toms—took up defensive positions along the deck with their Krags. Captain Gringo didn't blame them. He was sure they were invisible from the shore right now, blacked out against the dark eastern sky. But the compound was bigger than he'd expected, and worse yet, there was little or no cover for a landing party.

A little scrub grew here and there in patches on the flat coral island—not enough to hide more than one or two behind in any one place. So, yeah, it would have to be a frontal attack against at least one machine-gun position, if and when. He still might be able to talk the princess and her people out of it.

He climbed out of the cockpit for a better look, and spotted improvised thatched shelters beyond the tin roofs and guard tower. He muttered, "Okay, the prisoners are out of our line of attack if we're careful about plunging fire. But where the hell are the docking facilities you mentioned, Hilda? I don't see any landing place. The effing waves are just washing in along the whole windward beach."

She said, "I'm not sure this ist the island we landed on, Dick. It looks like it, aber in some ways it *doesn't*! Could not there be *two* pearl-diving operations out here?"

"I had to ask. Okay, I've seen what there is to see, here at least. Let's get out of here, Alberto!"

The man at the helm grinned and said that sounded like a hell of a good idea. Then, as Alberto swung the helm hard over, he died, and so did some of the others, when machine-gun fire raked La Paloma from stem to stern!

Beatriz shouted, "Man the Maxim, Deek!" as she grabbed the helm to swing it hard over the other way, keeping her head down as more hot lead smashed into the cabin bulkhead just above it. Captain Gringo ran forward as the gunner of the steam launch that had been shadowing them astern lent wings to his heels by chewing up the deck behind him. Then he dropped behind his own machine gun as Beatriz, bless her, swung La Paloma broadside to the approaching steam launch.

The other pilot didn't seem to care. He steered to ram the lugger amidships with his metal-sheathed bow as Captain Gringo, ignoring that for the moment, drew a bead on the winking muzzle flare of the other automatic weapon and opened up with his own.

The results were more than he'd hoped for. The blackbirders hadn't expected another machine gun aboard what looked like simply a nosy fishing boat. So he ploughed them good from stem to stern with point-blank raking fire. The other gunner in the bows was blown back from the breechblock of his Spandau as more rounds punched holes in the steam boiler amidships. The boiler did what any high-pressure boiler would do with holes punched in it. It blew up, scalding hell out of anyone that hadn't already been shot. One plate blew out through the launch's hull just below the water line. So as it fell dead in the water, it also proceeded to turn turtle.

Everyone aboard La Paloma should have been cheering about now. But nobody was, and someone was calling Beatriz a stupid cow. Captain Gringo tore his gaze from the sinking launch, and while "cow" seemed a little cruel, he understood why everyone seemed so upset. La Paloma was headed directly ashore, and on shore, guys were running around like the ants of a stomped nest, shouting in German and waving rifles in the limelit glare they were sailing right into!

He didn't yell back at Beatriz. He knew the poor kid was doing her best to do almost anything else as breakers broke over the stern, driving the lugger aground in the shallows. He dropped below, scooped up more ammo boxes, and lobbed them up on deck. Then he climbed out and started hauling the tripod out of the deck planking as, yeah, the first mortar round from somewhere ashore keened over the lugger to explode astern. *Just* astern!

It didn't take a degree in military science to see the

disadvantages of remaining on a stationary target while at least one mortar was ranging on it. So he had lots of company in the bow as he finished tugging the gun mount free. A couple of guys had already jumped overboard to struggle shoreward in the chest-high surf. One had even thought to keep his rifle. Beatriz dropped to her bare knees by Captain Gringo, sobbing, "I *tried*! I could not beat back out to sea against the wind and surf!"

He said, "I noticed. Grab a couple of ammo boxes and follow me."

She did. Atanua had made it close enough to catch the last order as well. So as he waded ashore with the Maxim held high, the two girls followed with at least four boxes of ammo in addition to the belt he'd already reloaded with. The only problem, now, was what the fuck he was supposed to *do* with it!

As they waded ashore and dropped behind the biggest clump of brush they could find, one of the crewmen who'd beaten them ashore was walking toward the limelight with his hands held high in surrender, shouting for mercy. He didn't get much. A fusillade of rifle fire cut him down like a dog.

Captain Gringo set up his Maxim, armed it, and as others crowded in behind the same clump, yelled, "Spread out, hit the dirt, and use your own guns, damn it! Make them work at nailing us all with the same mortar round!"

Most of them could see the sense of that. As he growled, "Beatriz, we've soldiered together before, so you're my loader. Atanua, keep your head up and your ass down, here, on my other side."

The Kanaka girl said, "Me got rifle dropped by sissy. Who you wantem me shoot? Whattafuck's going on?"

"Cover my right flank and shoot anything trying to come down the beach at us." He sighed as, to his left, Beatriz gasped, "Eleven o'clock, Deek!"

He swung the muzzle to cover the rifle squad charging them bold as brass, outlined by the camp lights, but held his fire as Beatriz insisted, "Shoot! For why are you waiting, Deek?"

He let them get within point-blank range before he mowed them flat in a moaning windrow and said quietly, "That's why. Where are Hilda and Alfrieda?"

Beatriz said she hadn't seen them leave the lugger. So when, a few seconds later, the mortar landed a round directly on the stranded craft and, having the range now, proceeded to pound La Paloma to kindling, he shook his head wearily and said, "Shit, they were both great kissers, too!"

Then Atanua said, "Somebody creeping at us. But they vahines alleesame me, my word. Hey, they German sistahs!"

Captain Gringo turned and called out, "Hilda, over here on the double! We thought you kids were dead!"

The bedraggled blonde said, "Ach, we thought so, too!" as she and the redhead joined them in the now most meager cover. Alfrieda said something in German. Hilda translated and said, "She ist right. She a stockholder in Halle und Feldmacher ist. So they would not shoot her!"

He pointed with his chin at one of the still forms on the chalky ground out front and growled, "I wouldn't bet on that. They just blew away old Padilla without asking him what he might or might not own stock in."

"But, Dick, if a woman approached them waving a white cloth . . ."

"Okay, so then what?"

"We could maybe a deal machen?"

"What deal could we offer them? They've got us pinned down with our backs to the sea. They know better now than to charge us. But we sure as shit ain't about to charge them, and once the moon rises, they'll be able to pick us off with that mortar. They'd be lobbing at us right now if they didn't care about wasting ammo. Hey, that's a bright note. They may not have an unlimited amount of ammo. On the other hand, neither have *we*!''

Alfrieda said something that sounded pretty firm and reached out to snatch Atanua's light-colored tapa cloth from around her hips. The vahine gasped, ''Hey, whassamatter you? This no time to play feely-feely, dumb Haole cunt!''

But the redhead had risen and stepped into the light, waving the tapa wildly, before anyone could stop her. Captain Gringo yelled, ''Come back here, dammit!'' as the redhead strode toward the unseen enemy, shouting in German. A distant male voice called out to her. Hilda said, ''Ach, so! I thought they would agree to parley!'' And then *she* was up and away as Captain Gringo muttered, ''Oh shit!''

Beatriz asked, ''Do you think those Germans will rape them before they execute them?'' in a surprisingly complacent tone. He looked around, spotted a clump not much smaller than the one they were behind, and said, ''Both of you move straight back to the berm of the beach. Then crawl for that clump to our south while I cover you.''

''But why, Dick? Do you think they have this cover spotted?''

''*Move!* Damn it!''

So they moved. He waited until nobody on either side was in sight, then moved himself, just in time. He'd no sooner set up behind the other cover before the clump they'd been behind when the German girls proceeded to get mowed flat with mortar fire, at least ten rounds.

A few minutes later, a skirmish line of roughly dressed scouts came charging out against the light, yelling like boisterous teenagers, in Spanish. Captain Gringo let them make it to the flattened target area so his muzzle flash wouldn't show from the watchtower as he mowed them down in turn.

Beatriz said, "Hey, they did not sound like Germans, Dick!" and he replied, "They weren't. Why send a friend when you can send a cheap stooge? We knew they'd hired Costa Rican toughs. That's why they're so casual about expending them. The mothers I want are out of range, and they'll probably stay there. It's been nice knowing you, girls. But once the moon comes up, we've had it!"

Beatriz sighed and asked, "Could we make love one time before I must die, Deek?"

"I thought you were in mourning."

"I am. For me. I have been free for to make love to you for almost an hour, and it looks as if I shall never see the dawn with any man again!"

"We're not licked yet," he lied, looking around until he spotted one of their own guys flattened out behind another smaller clump. He called out, "Hey, Pedro, if you slid back and rolled over the berm, you might make it into the shallows."

The crewman replied, "That is true, Captain Gringo, but then what? I do not think I can swim a hundred nautical miles against the wind, do you?"

"No, but if you could make it around to the far side where the South Sea Islanders are being held, with a message—"

"Forget it," Pedro replied flatly, adding: "In the first place, I do not speak their tongue. In the second, suicide is against my religion, and those limelights reach well out to sea in all directions. Further out than I wish for to swim at night in shark-infested waters!"

The naked Atanua said, "Goddam, whassamatter you, Dick? *Me* can swim like fishy fishy and talk Kanaka like native, too!"

He shook his head and said, "Too risky, Honey. He's

right about sharks. That light should have 'em cruising just outside the breakers, curious as hell.''

"Pooh, I told you my people friends with Kai, and if me no go now, goddam Hina, you call her 'Moon,' come up and we all be dead anyway! What you want island boys do, Dick?''

"Jesus, *anything*! There's no way we're about to be rescued by the U.S. Cavalry out here. Not even Gaston could have the Orotiki here in less than ten or twenty hours, even if he knew we needed help. But if the prisoners could cause some kind of diversion, or at least douse those damned lights—''

"Okeedokee," she cut in, springing up to dash bare-ass toward the sea. It was a bad move. Someone opened up on her from the guard tower, but though bullets splashed all about her bare ass as she waded out, she was gone before they could range on her. In what must have been sheer frustration, the blackbirders lobbed a mortar round at her last known position as well. Captain Gringo growled, "Thank you very much, Squarehead. Now that we know your tower's in telephone communication with the masked mortar battery, we can—Shit, no we can't.''

Beatriz said, "She is most brave. I forgive her for having had you first. Do you think she will make it, Deek?''

He shrugged and said, "She might. For all the difference it can make, unless they at least knock those lights out. Have you been keeping your pretty head against bulkheads lately, Querida?''

She fluttered her lashes and asked, "What else was there to do when one was the mujer of a man who did not really make full use of her? Oh, how I wish I had been able to join that party, Deek. Do you think there is any chance at all of there ever being another?''

Before he could reassure her with a white lie, one of the

other pinned-down Costa Ricans sobbed, "Jesus, Maria y Jose! Look what's coming now!"

Captain Gringo turned his gaze seaward, staring steadily, too resigned to even swear as, just offshore, the German gunboat Seeshlange ran up the white battle flag of Der Kaiser and a loudspeaker started roaring out across the water.

He sighed and said, "Dumb bastards must not be able to speak Spanish." Then the same loudspeaker bellowed, in German-accented Spanish, "All of you, lay down your arms in the name of Der Kaiser! The game is up, and it will go hard with you all if you do not surrender at once!"

Captain Gringo stayed right where he was. But the nearby Pedro sprang to his feet, hands up, only to be shot in the back and flop right down again.

Beatriz sighed and said, "They mean to show no mercy?" and all he could come up with was, "Why should they?"

The turrets of the big gray gunboat began to swing ominously as the loudspeaker bellowed, "So?" which meant about the same in German or Spanish. Then all hell broke loose as the Seeshlange started throwing salvo after salvo of no-kidding 155 H.E!

Captain Gringo had flattened Beatriz in the sand and rolled atop her to screen her from shrapnel at least. So it took him a few seconds of sheer terror to realize that, though the earth was quivering under them like jelly, the gunboat's rounds were landing too far off for a guy to be pissing his pants like this. He raised his head gingerly and gasped, "I'll be damned, they're not ranging on us! They're firing on the blackbirders and, oh beautiful! There goes the guard tower and, yep, there go the lights!"

But you couldn't fool the Kriegsmarine with a little blackout. A star shell exploded high above the small island to light up every target as it swung from its paper parachute. The gunboat lobbed more 155s and another flare. Then someone had the brains to run up a white flag, plainer than the one the gunboat was flying, and the loudspeaker roared in both German and Spanish, "Very well, we are sending marine infantry ashore to disarm one and all. It will go hard on anyone they find with even an umbrella in his hands!"

They sounded as though they meant it. So Captain Gringo got up from behind the machine gun as the last flare went out. He helped Beatriz to her feet and said, "Let's move right to the water's edge. I don't want them mixing us with those other guys, do you?"

She said, "Deek, I wet myself just now. I was so frightened."

He laughed and said, "Welcome to the club, Soldada." Then he called out to his other few survivors and led the girl into waist-deep water to at least kill the smell of their duds below their now less nervous bladders.

A whaleboat ground ashore nearby, and a couple of guys who looked as if they couldn't make up their minds about being soldiers or sailors leaped out at them, pointing rifles and apparently calling them awful names in German. Captain Gringo and the girl raised their hands, hoping that would do it. Then a voice snapped an order in the same language and the marine infantry moved on inland as Von Linderhoff, now in a white tropic officer's kit, climbed out to say, "So, Captain Gringo, we meet again."

The tall American said, "Yeah, and I never thought I'd be so glad to see *you*! Would you mind telling us what the fuck's going *on* here?"

Von Linderhoff turned to yell some more orders at another boat landing farther down the beach. Then he moved closer, saying, "I thought it so obvious, Walker. Didn't I tell you chattel slavery was against the law in all civilized countries?"

"Yeah, but I didn't know yours was quite that civilized.

Why the hell were you trying to scare us off if *you* were after the blackbirders, too?''

The sardonic one-eyed German stared past them at the smoking chaos in the center of the island and said, ''That, also, would have been obvious to anyone but a wild man like yourself! Look at the stupid mess you just got yourself into, biting off more than you could chew, as usual!''

He nodded politely at Beatriz and added curtly, ''Also I see, as usual, you have dragged innocent bystanders into the quicksand with you! Why could not you have taken friendly advice just once?''

''You call all those attempts to knock me and my friends off friendly *advice*, you cold-blooded Kraut?''

''What are you raving about now? I told you to get out of my case because it was my case and I had orders to handle it *delicately*, not like *this*, goddamn it! Halle und Feldmacher is, as you know, a German firm, with stockholders in high places. But they were as crazy as you, so once two of my field agents were murdered by their hired killers, I was able to convince headquarters it was time to take the gloves off, nicht wahr?''

Captain Gringo swallowed a green taste as he decided not to explain just who he might or might not have killed, himself, until he knew who they were talking about. He asked, ''Are you saying you had no agents out to do anything but scare off Princess Manukai and me?''

Von Linderhoff turned to wave another boatload of marine infantry in to the mop-up before he looked disgusted and told Captain Gringo, ''I had none of my agents after you at *all*, once we found out what you thought you were up to and we'd had our little talk. Halle und Feldmacher seem to have had a whole army of hired guns out trying to hang on here until the end of this year's pearling season, at least. I had two of my best men watching a couple of them at the same hotel the princess checked into. Somehow, the company agents got the advantage and murdered them both as they were apparently following someone who'd contacted the girls.''

"Right, two sisters from Bremerhaven named Hilda and Alfrieda.''

"They were not sisters. They were secret agents for Halle und Feldmacher. But how did *you* know this, Walker?''

"I sort of guessed it, even before someone shelled the last position they'd seen me in. They sailed out with us, hoping to lead us astray among the desert isles to the north. Your shore party should be bringing them in any time now. I can't wait to hear old Hilda try and wiggle out of this one.''

"Nothing they say will do them any good, now that they have been involved in the murder of two German field agents. You are lucky to be alive yourself. They are both very wicked girls.''

"I noticed. Let's get back to all the bombings and ambushes. I'll take your word it wasn't the work of your guys. This is the second time you've had me at your mercy and I'm still alive. But if we assume the guys trying to stop the rescue party from Konakona, rough, were Halle und Feldmacher, who was acting *spooky*, you?''

"Do I look like a prankster, damn it?''

"Not really. I guess we can write that off as island politics. Some rivals at the court on Konakona wanted to scare the princess off—to keep her from looking good, not because they gave a fig about peasant pearl divers—and, yeah, killing her all the way might strike them as tapu. So it works, sort of, and now that the captives have been freed, I hope—''

Von Linderhoff cut in, "What do you mean, you hope? Don't you think we had range charts aboard that ship out there? Naturally we avoided shelling the side of this island the natives are being held. I told you we were having

enough trouble with Samoan chiefs who have been lied to
about us by the British and French!''

As he spied a familiar figure coming their way, escorted
by two burly Kanakas and a bemused German marine
infantryman, he called Atanua over; and when the stark-
naked vahine was formally introduced to Von Linderhoff,
she turned back to Captain Gringo and said, ''My word,
whatta swim and whatta nice kuluau we makem them
blackbirder pricks! When me tellum prisoners you say time
to rushem guards, they rushem *good,* my word!''

Von Linderhoff questioned the marine infantry noncom
and apparently found the German version more understandable. He smiled thinly at Captain Gringo and said, ''Very
well, you are forgiven after all. I told you I had orders to
handle this matter delicately. The enslaved natives seem to
have, ah, liquidated the survivors of our drum-fire.''

''You call that a delicate ending?''

''Of course. If nobody has to stand *trial,* the case is
closed! The company directors back in Bremerhaven will
of course disavow any knowledge of blackbirding, and
from now on be more discreet, nicht wahr?''

Captain Gringo turned back to Atanua and asked if
she'd seen any sign of Hilda or Alfrieda in the overrun
enemy camp. The vahine sighed and said, ''Sure, signs of
both, all over the place. My word, shell musta landed on
'em going sixty-nine!''

He swallowed again and told Von Linderhoff, ''I guess
that's that, then. What happens now?''

The German said, ''Naturally, you shall all be landed
safely back on Costa Rican soil. I assume the princess will
have room for the natives Der Kaiser just rescued from a
life of slavery?''

''Sure. That's what she brought the schooner from
Konakona to do in the first place. So, in a weird way, it
looks my side *won* this time!''

• • •

The return trip to Puntarenas aboard the Seeshlange was much faster but still sort of tedious. The spoilsport square-heads insisted on the antiseptic separation of sexes and kept telling the natives singing songs of joy in the hold to shut up. Worse yet, they had one of the new Marconi wireless sets on the bridge to play with. So though Marconi was probably full of it when he said that someday people would be able to chat across a whole ocean, the dots and dashes made it to the mainland ahead of them, and as they steamed into the harbor the next day, the whole damned town seemed to be waiting on the quay for them. There hadn't been as much excitement since the last earthquake, and the German consulate had even sent a brass band to oomp-pa-pa at everyone.

Atanua was still in the hold with the other "naked primitives" as the German crew dropped the gangplank to the landing. But Captain Gringo saw Beatriz on deck and grabbed her, saying, "Let's get out of here poco tiempo. Von Linderhoff's okay, but some of the people he works for can be officious as hell and I'm not sure our passports are in order!"

Nobody tried to stop them as they were first ashore. Von Linderhoff had told them not to. So Captain Gringo and the girl made it to the less-crowded quay running the length of the waterfront—before the pier the gunboat was tied up to could get really crowded.

Gaston intercepted them halfway to the Orotiki, saying, "Eh bien, we heard. The princess is threatening to give a luau on deck, whatever that means, and any press photographers not snapping pictures of the très heroic German liberators at the moment will be aboard the schooner taking pictures of tits. It is apparently permissible to print pictures of tits if the people displaying them are dark and quaint enough, hein?''

Captain Gringo muttered, ''Jesus, I don't want them taking pictures of my quaint *face,* either!''

''Oui, those reward-poster portraits culled from your old West Point yearbook already look enough like you. That is why I dashed madly to meet you.''

''You dashed right. Did you bring our payoff as well?''

''Mais non. As I said, the princess is so excited by the rescue I have not been able to sit her down long enough to discuss business. I confess I was très overjoyed, myself, when the news came in ahead of you. But there are limits to how long a man my age can dash about kissing people, and when one reconsiders, it was no big thing, as Kuruhai keeps saying. I must say that for once you did things neatly and avec less of the usual noise, hein?''

''It was noisy enough.'' Captain Gringo sighed, putting a comforting arm around Beatriz's shoulders as he added, ''We still have to settle up with this lady and the other Costa Rican survivors for losing them their boat. So go back to the schooner and tell Manukai she owes extra. You can work the exact amount out with her. She owes us for the lugger itself, and some compensation for the families of, let's see . . . four guys. We didn't manage to get any women on our side killed, thank God.''

Gaston nodded and said, ''Eh bien, Manukai is très lousy with money, and I'll point out how much we saved her. Where will I find you two when the tedious finances are settled, at the posada?''

Captain Gringo shook his head and said, ''There could still be some sore losers left over from Halle und Feldmacher. But the suite Manukai booked at the Casa Real was paid for a week in advance and, what the hell, *she* won't be using it anymore.''

Gaston laughed and said, "Eh bien, I admire your thrift, and it's not a bad four-poster. Plenty of room for *normal* sized people. What about the machine guns?"

"The Germans wouldn't give me back the Maxim for some reason. Had a hell of a time hanging on to my thirty-eight. Did you ever get that Browning back in shape?"

"Oui, and I am still très cross at you about that, Dick. After all the trouble I had cleaning it and setting it up on the poop, I never got to use it. My question was, Is the remaining machine gun ours or theirs?"

"Let 'em keep it. We'd look silly checking machine guns into hotels, and they could still run into trouble getting all those natives safely home. Be sure you knock when you catch up with us at the Hotel Casa Real."

Gaston chuckled fondly and left them to their own devices. Beatriz seemed thrilled at the thought of checking into a grand hotel with a handsome Americano. He felt less excited. But he owed the poor little mutt a few days of luxurious slap and tickle before they left her behind and, what the hell, it wasn't as if the pretty little mestiza figured to be a tedious bed partner. He could tell her boilers were building up a head of steam even before they got to the hotel.

Getting through the lobby of a posh hotel with a lady of dark complexion and ragged-ass peon costume was a little complicated, however. Captain Gringo placed a generous tip on the marble counter as he explained to the room clerk that they both worked for the Princess Manukai and that she'd said it was okay. The clerk started to tell them to go to hell, took a second look at the banknotes by the hotel register, and spun the big book around, saying, "I suppose it will be all right, provided you sign in under the name of your employer, Senor."

As Captain Gringo did so, the clerk handed him the key.

The tall American took it. Then he took a second look at Manukai's childish signature, snapped his fingers, and said, "Oh hell, of course!"

He moved Beatriz out of earshot, handed her the key, and said, "Go up and wait for me, Querida. I gotta get Gaston off that tub poco tiempo!"

Then he headed for the door without explaining further. He was moving as fast as one could in a hotel lobby without causing a panic, so Beatriz, smart girl, simply headed for the stairs to do what she'd been told.

Outside, though broad day, a guy could move faster. So he did. He was jogging toward the waterfront when he saw Atanua, wearing a mumu for a change, running all-out toward *him*. He kept going as they met. The vahine fell in beside him and gasped, "Whattafuckee going on? Gaston whisper on me to go gettem you just before skipper order everybody but ship's officers and some new crew just come aboard below. Me slippem ashore instead. Why Princess Manukai want everybody, even Gaston, down in hold, Dick?"

He grunted, "To kill them, of course. Manukai's not Manukai. God knows where the rival faction found her, but everything just fell in place when I saw her handwriting doesn't match the official signature of the real princess! You say all the people we saved and all the people you know personally from back home are locked below decks out of the way?"

"Sure, even Makomotu. Whuffo they wanna lockem even ship's mate in hold with crew, Dick?"

"Because he's honest as well as dumb. Don't you get it yet? Your king sent his daughter, the crown princess, on a mission that makes her kid brother, the sissy crown prince, look like, well, a sissy. So his pals at court plan a double-cross. They've already, no doubt, murdered the real Manukai and buried her someplace. That Chinese cook should bob to the surface of the harbor any day now. All their odd moves, from hiring two known wild men like Gaston and me, to mysterious and only apparent attempts on that substitute-Manukai's life have been razzle-dazzle bullshit they wanted the court back on Konakona to hear about. Because at some point in the proceedings, they've intended all along to fake the more public murder of the princess by the blackbirders!''

"Tangaroa's toenails! Blackbirders not bad enough, they gottem killem *princess*?''

"They might not have gotten to, if her co-heir's sneaks hadn't simply murdered her and made the switch, to keep a sissy's she-male rival from looking good! They may have had other reasons for wanting the mission to fail. The German company played rough, but they did insist they had valid labor contracts for those pearl divers they were holding; and I know at least one German who tells the truth once in a while. So if I can get any of you good guys back to Konakona alive, it might be interesting to have the king look into just who betrayed some of his people into slavery!''

"Hot shit, s'pose King Kamamamoku find out Prince Tinirau big shit alongside big sissy, Tinirau gonna wind up *cooked*! Why we runnem up this side street, Dick? Schooner *that* way, no?''

"I know where the Orotiki is. You keep going at the next corner, and don't stop until you reach the police station two blocks farther. Get Police Captain Herrerra. He's okay. Tell him I need a mess of cops on the double, and not to worry about any noise he hears on the way to the docks!''

Again, not waiting to see if the lady was carrying out his instructions, Captain Gringo cut south along an alley to hit the waterfront from the dark slit lined up with the gangplank of the Orotiki. As Atanua had said, there were only a dozen-odd guys on deck, and they were making ready to shove off. But mercifully, as he'd hoped, they were still waiting for the turn of the tide.

There was no way for a visible man to cross the quay without being spotted. So as he ran for the gangplank, the fake princess, standing on the poop, saw him coming and screamed an order in Kanaka.

But by the time the two guys amidship were grabbing the other end of the gangplank, Captain Gringo was halfway up it, shooting .38 slugs to discourage them from acting so inhospitable. He nailed one in the head and spun the other to the deck too badly wounded to argue about who might or might not come aboard.

But as the tall American ran aft, others started shooting at him from every direction. He made it up the ladder to the poop anyway, and dove over a skylight to land rolling and crab sideways behind the wheelbox as the skylight glass evaporated in a hail of wild gunfire.

He reloaded his pistol as he got his bearings, bullets thunking into the wheelbox between him and the rest of the vessel. He saw the tarp-covered Browning Gaston had set up atop a nearby hatchway. But not *that* nearby, damn it.

As he started crawling toward it, keeping below the level of the shot-up skylight, he saw Manukai, or whoever she was, sprawled on the deck ahead, oozing a lot. As he reached his free hand out to touch hers, she opened one eye and gasped weakly, "What happened? Who put out the sun?"

He said, "Never yell 'Fire' without getting the hell out of the way, Doll. Where are you hit?"

"All over, I think. Why the hell did they shoot *me*? That wasn't the way Kuruhai said it was supposed to turn out, damn it."

"Never mind what he promised you. Was he the ringleader?"

She didn't answer. She didn't have to. He pulled her in by her dead wrist, sliding her along the deck on her own blood, and with some effort rolled her up atop the skylight frame. A bullet thunked into her big corpse. Then someone on the other side recognized her mumu and they stopped shooting her for now. Captain Gringo took a deep breath as he gathered his knees under him. Then he jumped up, grabbed the Browning from its mount, and took cover behind his improvised fort of dead female flesh before they could shoot him as well.

He hastily unwrapped the Browning to find that Gaston, bless him, had armed the machine gun with three full belts linked together. Better yet, he heard a police whistle in the distance, ashore. So bless Atanua and Captain Herrerra, too.

Now the traitors had at least one flank as well as him to worry about. So enough of this pussyfooting. He cranked a round into the chamber with the arming lever, got to his feet with the Browning braced on his right hip, and proceeded to spray everyone in sight aboard the schooner with full-automatic fire!

He only blew away two-thirds of them as panic-stricken Kanakas armed only with Krags or, worse, pistols, wasted time pegging wild shots back at him instead of taking cover poco tiempo. Those smart enough to get a mast or solid hunk of superstructure between them and the chattering death machine blasting down from the poop didn't really do that much better. For Herrerra of the Puntarenas P.D. was an old pal of Captain Gringo's who was smart enough to assume, correctly, that anyone Captain Gringo was shooting at had to be a bad guy. So he ordered his squad of carbine-packing cops to lay down a withering flanking fire from shore, and in no time everyone in the gang who wasn't grabbing for some sky and screaming for mercy was flat on the deck making messy red puddles of blood mixed with piss.

Captain Gringo dropped the hot Browning and met the cops on the main deck as they came warily aboard. Herrerra said, ''I know Costa Rica has no extradition treaty with any of the countries that want you. But I still hope you have an explanation for all this. What did we just do?''

The American said, ''You just saved this vessel from sinking offshore with a mess of innocents locked in the hold! You and your men figure to get a mess of citations and probably a reward from the king of Konakona if you'll only be kind enough to do all the paperwork. I'm just not up to it.''

He saw Kuruhai among the prisoners the local cops were herding toward him and their superior. It figured. He said, ''Okay, Skipper. You were just about to unlock that padlock and lift the hatch for us, right?''

Kuruhai shrugged and said, ''Ain't no big thing, Blalah. This whole deal was Princess Manukai's idea. I just work here, see?''

''Bullshit! She was too stupid to plot her next meal, and if she ever got through Vassar I'm a graduate of Peking University! You just found a big dumb broad who looked enough like the real princess to fool commoners who'd never gotten close enough to the tapu real thing to matter. You and the prince you were working for planned to make it look as if the real princess had been killed on a mission the sissy said would never succeed. And now you're about to unlock that hold for us, aren't you?''

As the treacherous skipper knelt at their feet, Captain Herrerra asked, ''Do we have murder in the first degree on this hombre? I enjoy arresting murderers. But can we *prove* it?''

Captain Gringo said, "Sure. He's going to give you a full confession, tell you where the real princess was disposed of, and take his chances with a Costa Rican court. Ain't that right, Kuruhai?"

The big Kanaka sobbed and cursed in his own language as he unlocked the hold. Captain Gringo chuckled and told Herrerra, "Costa Rica only *executes* murderers. I understand justice is a little grimmer in some parts of the South Pacific."

Then he saw Atanua coming aboard, smiling with delight at the carnage all around, and added, "Speaking of the South Pacific . . ."

As Kuruhai opened the hatch and bewildered natives started climbing out, the vahine clapped her hands and said, "Oh, you savem allee nice and killem allee bad, big sweet cock! How we ever thank you?"

He said, "Easy. You have enough honest able-bodied seamen to get this tub back to Konakona with the king's captured subjects and what's left of his money. You'll tell him what really happened, and I imagine he'll know what to do about the traitors at his court."

Gaston had emerged from the hatch, blinking, just in time to hear mention of money. He said, "It's about time you got here, Dick. Merci, M'selle Atanua. But as to our just reward . . ."

Captain Gringo drew him aside and muttered, "Let's get the fuck out of here while everyone's too happy to wonder about the money we already helped ourselves to! I know we were promised more, and I know we sure as hell earned it. But there are times it's better to quit while you're ahead, and Herrerra's already bending the rules for us!"

Gaston headed for the gangplank with him, but said, "Merde alors, such a rude child. You should learn not to interrupt your elders. I was just about to say that, before they turned on me, I was forced to spend most of the time you were away in Manukai's cabin, and my tongue will never recover. But from time to time, the orgasmic monstress slept, and as she did so I got into her sea chest, as a refreshing change from her cunt.''

''You grabbed our dough?''

''I grabbed as much as I could tuck discreetly in my pockets. Who counts gold coins in the dark, hein? If I took too much, we and our friends earned that too, non?''

Captain Gringo laughed and said, ''Let's get the hell away before anyone looks at the books, if there are any books. I'm shacked up at the hotel, as I said I'd be. I, ah, don't think Beatriz goes for three in a boat.''

Gaston shrugged and replied, ''Merde alors, I have too romantique a nature for the sloppiness of seconds when I have something else lined up. So let me give you your share, and when the coast is clear you can look me up at Mamma Rosa's, hein?''

As they divided the money in a shaded doorway, Captain Gringo said, ''I guess the posada should be safe enough now. But don't you know any dames in town who have their own quarters, Gaston?''

''But of course I do. Rosa owns the whole posada, non?''

''Jesus, you mean to shack up with Mamma Rosa herself?''

''Why not, now that we know she charges nothing for screwing like a mink and that her body bears no relation at all to her somewhat careworn face?''

They shook on it and parted friendly. But Captain Gringo was laughing to himself at the mental picture as he headed back to the hotel and the much younger and prettier Beatriz. Then, since he was only human and he *had* seen Mamma Rosa in the buff that time, he wound up laughing even harder when he caught himself wondering if he could just possibly be missing out on something good.